BEFORE SHE KNEW WHAT WAS HAPPENING, HE WAS kissing her. Just like that. As if he had every reason and right in the world to do so. And not small kisses of comfort on her cheek and eyes as he used to do when she was younger, but deep kisses, filled with longing and desire. The very suddenness and unexpectedness of it all prevented her from putting up any sort of guard against him, and seven years of estrangement dissolved in an instant.

Everything about him was so familiar. His hard mouth, his skillful lips—she remembered and responded to it all. He tasted of brandy, fire, and danger, even more danger than she'd felt earlier tonight when they were being shot at. But she was unable to do anything but return his kisses with an ever-increasing fervor. She hadn't felt this way in so long, as if there were nothing in the world more important than this moment. His darkly erotic scent was like an aphrodisiac to her, making her weaker until she was clinging to him, making her stronger until she was wordlessly demanding more.

Her hand slipped along his shoulder to the back of his neck. Then, sliding off the band that held his hair, her fingers glided up to bring his lips down on hers harder. It worked. Thank God, it worked. He thrust his tongue, reaching deep into her mouth until she moaned with satisfaction. Heat gathered in all parts of her, burning away her bad memories, liquefying her bones and her resolve.

WHAT ARE *LOVESWEPT* ROMANCES?

They are stories of true romance and touching emotion. We believe those two very important ingredients are constants in our highly sensual and very believable stories in the LOVESWEPT line. Our goal is to give you, the reader, stories of consistently high quality that may sometimes make you laugh, sometimes make you cry, but are always fresh and creative and contain many delightful surprises within their pages.

Most romance fans read an enormous number of books. Those they truly love, they keep. Others may be traded with friends and soon forgotten. We hope that each LOVESWEPT romance will be a treasure—a "keeper." We will always try to publish

LOVE STORIES YOU'LL NEVER FORGET
BY AUTHORS YOU'LL ALWAYS REMEMBER

The Editors

Loveswept ® 908

The Damaron Mark:
THE
LOVERS

FAYRENE
PRESTON

BANTAM BOOKS
NEW YORK · TORONTO · LONDON · SYDNEY · AUCKLAND

THE DAMARON MARK: THE LOVERS
A Bantam Book / October 1998

ISBN 0-553-44535-9

Published simultaneously in the United States and Canada

*Bantam Books are published by Bantam Books, a division of Bantam
Doubleday Dell Publishing Group, Inc. Its trademark, consisting of the
words "Bantam Books" and the portrayal of a rooster, is Registered in U.S.
Patent and Trademark Office and in other countries. Marca Registrada.
Bantam Books, 1540 Broadway, New York, New York 10036.*

PRINTED IN THE UNITED STATES OF AMERICA

OPM   10 9 8 7 6 5 4 3 2 1

ONE

When the door of her office opened, Kylie Damaron didn't bother to look up from the papers she was studying. "Did you find that new information, Clifford?"

"I don't know who Clifford is," came a low, deep drawl. "I also don't have a clue where the new information is. But I'm willing to bet that Clifford will get it to you ASAP or die trying."

Kylie stilled at the sound of the familiar voice.

Slowly, she raised her head and encountered the golden-eyed gaze of David Galado, the only person in the world besides a Damaron who would be allowed to bypass security and her assistants and walk into her office unannounced.

With his presence, electricity filled her office. She felt it against her skin as a heated pressure and she felt it inside her body as a shock of nerves. And there was nothing she could do about it.

She watched as he moved toward her with that distinctive, fluid, catlike grace that was unique to him, threading in and out of the numerous baskets and large bouquets of flowers without disturbing so much as a petal.

His grace was all the more unusual because he was a big man, his shoulders wide and his body hard with muscles he hadn't earned in a gym, but in combat situations around the world. No doubt he had moved much the same way during the years he'd spent in South America, weaving through steamy jungles, tracking down druglords.

David was an operative for an organization that officially didn't exist. She never knew where he was, or if and when he was coming home. Seven years ago, she'd convinced herself that it was better that way. Of course, she hadn't taken into account the effect he would have on her every time he suddenly appeared, the effect that was roughly the equivalent of a mild heart attack.

"It looks as if you've opened a florist shop," he said. "My invitation to the grand opening must have gotten lost in the mail."

She eyed him warily. "Well, you know how it is."

"No, I'm not sure I do. Why don't you tell me."

She shrugged. "It's hard to depend on the mail these days, or, for that matter, anything or anyone."

He grinned, but no humor reached his eyes. "Now that you mention it, I've noticed that too. Sad, isn't it?"

"I suppose it would be sad for someone if they were the type who depended on others. I don't. Not anymore."

"How interesting. Does that mean you've had yourself hermetically sealed?"

Silence, she belatedly decided, would be best in this situation until she found out what he wanted. And knowing him as well as she did, she seriously doubted that he'd stopped by her office to shoot the breeze. Something was definitely up, but she couldn't even begin to guess what.

David was a member of the Damarons' extended family—their great-aunt Abigail, the matriarch of their family, was his godmother—and he'd been in her life for practically as long as she could remember.

She'd once viewed him as a close friend, confidant, and protector. Then, as she'd grown older, she'd fallen in love with him. Her love had lasted until the morning after her twenty-first birthday.

Since then, she coped with him by trying to keep as much distance between them as possible, even when they were in the same room, which happened once or twice a year. In those instances, as now, all she could do was try to keep her head and view him as objectively as she could.

But for the moment, until he decided to tell her what he wanted, she allowed herself the luxury of taking in everything she could about him. Today, a perfectly cut taupe suit graced his powerful body, and his long brown hair was pulled back from his face in a ponytail, bound at the nape of his neck. The style drew attention to his sharply cut cheekbones and the unusual golden color of his eyes.

Other than a few new lines on his face, she reflected, he hadn't changed a bit. He was still the exotic, elegant savage she'd privately named him long ago.

He strolled around the desk, pushed aside her

leather out box, then hitched one hip and a thigh on the corner of the desk so that he was facing her. "Hello, Kylie."

"David," she said levelly, though her heart leaped. He was too close. The magnetism he exuded so effortlessly felt as if it were reaching out for her, trying to pull her to him.

"It's good to see you made it home in one piece once more."

"Is it?"

"Why would you even question that?"

"Because the last time we spoke, you gave me the definite impression you weren't very happy with me."

"I wasn't."

" 'Happy' wouldn't describe the way *I* felt either."

Three months ago, after not talking with her for close to a year, he'd called her from his Paris hotel room. She had been en route by plane to the Wyoming vacation home of crime head Allesandro Molinari. Her purpose for the visit had been to get a vital piece of information for her cousin Wyatt. In a meeting the night before, her family had agreed that she should be the one to go. David, however, hadn't shared her family's faith in her. He had informed her in no uncertain terms that dealing with Molinari would be way over her head. Then he'd added insult to injury by telling her to have the pilot turn her plane around and head back home.

Now her instincts were telling her to get up and walk away from him, but she was surprised to find anger still simmering in her three months later. That anger, plus her pride, held her where she was. Using the three-inch heel of her shoe, she swiveled her high-backed leather chair around to meet his gaze directly. "Your attempted interference was completely out of line and I did *not* appreciate it."

He eyed her broodingly. " 'Attempted' is a good way to describe it. Unfortunately, my call didn't change a damn thing. You went right ahead and had the meeting anyway."

"Why not? I knew exactly what I was doing—a concept you couldn't seem to grasp at the time. But despite your doubts about my ability, I did an excellent job. I obtained the information Wyatt needed and everything went very smoothly."

"So I understand. From *Sin.*" There was a small crystal vase on her desk that contained five perfect roses, each a delicate peach color on the outside and a pale pink on the inside. He absently pulled one out and looked at it. "Why didn't you call me on your way back home as I had asked?"

She shrugged. "My first call had to go to Wyatt. My second call had to go to Sin so that he could inform the rest of the family. And since I left Wyoming later than I had originally planned, I simply decided it would be more convenient to have Sin call you, rather than wait until my flight home. That way, I ensured that you would get the news faster."

"Oh, I see—you were thinking of *me.*" He thrust the rose back into the vase with more energy than the task warranted and one soft, delicate petal floated down onto her desk, bruised.

"I chose the most expedient way to communicate with everyone, including you," she said, never once dropping her gaze from his. When she set her mind to it, she could keep her blue eyes clear no matter what she was thinking. Unfortunately, when she was with David, she had to put forth extra effort. The last thing she wanted him to know was that she'd never intended to call him back, nor did she want him to know how much he could still affect her. "I decided the faster you got the information, the faster you could rest easy and continue with your vacation, or whatever it was that you were doing in Paris."

"I appreciate your concern," he said with dry sarcasm. "However, I wouldn't have rested at all if I'd known you'd decided to spend three extra hours with Molinari."

She leaned back in her chair and studied him. The gold color of his eyes was so unusual, their intensity so strong, that whenever he went on one of his covert missions, he had to wear colored contacts. She'd once found several pairs in the bedroom that was his when he stayed with Abigail. And during the years he'd spent in South America, he'd worn his hair in Rastafarian braids rather than the sleek style he sported now. Despite his distinctive looks, David could be a chameleon when needed.

At the moment, his skin was the color of old copper instead of its normal golden beige, which told her his last mission had taken him to a place where the sun burned harsh and bright—the Middle East, more than likely. Of course, it could also mean that he'd spent a few weeks on vacation in some southern, exotic clime with a lithesome beauty.

But no, not this time. His face was all edges, his

body tensed. No, this time he'd just come off a mission. Obviously he'd gone straight from Paris back into a battle zone.

She had studied him from afar for so many years that she'd learned how to read certain things into his appearance and actions. But she'd never learned to read his mind.

"I wouldn't have stayed, David, if I'd sensed for one moment that I was in danger. Give me at least a *little* credit. I'm no longer that young girl you felt compelled to protect all those years ago."

His gaze swept slowly over her and heat flared in her wherever it touched.

"You don't think I know that?" he asked huskily.

"I think you sometimes forget."

Resting his forearm on his thigh, he leaned toward her. "Now, just *how* do you think I could erase the fact from my mind that you're a woman?"

No matter how hard she tried to suppress it, a blush rose beneath her ivory skin. Worse, he saw it, and satisfaction briefly flickered in his eyes.

She pushed up from her desk and walked around to the other side of it. "Look, this is a very unproductive conversation. All we're doing is rehashing something that happened three months ago, and it's over."

"If it's over, then why are you still seeing Molinari?"

"Because we enjoy each other's company."

Suddenly he was around her desk and standing in front of her. Close. *Extremely* close. But she couldn't seem to move away from him.

"It's instantly obvious why he enjoys your company," he said, his tone hard and biting. "Just look at you. What's not to enjoy?" He flicked at her hair, then, in a surprise move, allowed his fingers to linger among the fine strands. "Your hair—this baby blond stuff. This color never lasts through childhood—except with you."

"What's your point, David?" she asked somewhat breathlessly. It had been a long time since she'd been this close to him, but he hadn't changed. He was still fiercely male, with a potent sexuality and a darkly erotic scent emanating from his skin. Unwanted memories came flooding back to her, requiring her to use nearly all of her energy to block them from her mind.

"My *point*," he said through clenched teeth, "is that your hair color, along with the way you're wearing it now"—he swatted at the hair that brushed against her shoulders, then touched the hair that feathered around her face—"makes you look incredibly soft and vulnerable."

"Again I ask, what's your point?" This time she tried to move, but with the strength of his gaze and the light touch of his hand against the side of her neck, he kept her where she was.

"It's disarming as hell, that's what." With his hard, cutting tone and even harder face, he seemed almost on the edge of violence, but his touch was whisper soft as he slowly ran the back of his hand up and down her cheek, leaving behind a trail of heat. "And then there's this damn satin skin of yours."

He caressed the bare skin of her neck and arms, left exposed by the short-sleeved sheath she wore. He slid his hand down her arm, where he encircled his fingers around her slim wrist. "Look at this," he said. "These delicate bones could be snapped with no trouble at all."

It was fascinating to hear David describing her, because he'd rarely commented on her appearance over the years. There was something about his attitude that made his words sexually charged. And yet on the other hand, he was listing her assets so coolly, so objectively, he could have been looking at a horse.

"Hell, Kylie," he muttered, releasing her wrist with a light fling, "you know all of this as well as I do. Your beauty takes a man off guard and screws with his mind. You look fragile enough to break in his hands, and at the same time, you look sexy enough to come apart in his arms. Either way, it makes a man insane. Other than your business acumen—which I'll be the first to say is immense—it's the reason your cousins finally decided to agree to send you to Molinari's."

"David—"

He slid his hand around the back of her neck to hold her still, then leaned down until his mouth was inches away from hers and his warm breath feathered over her face. "You're a near-lethal combination, Kylie. Half the time a man doesn't know whether he wants to take you to bed and make love to you all night long, or to keep you by his side and protect you from all predators, including himself."

She circled out of his hold, then, with more space between them, she turned to face him. "Maybe men do want to protect me," she said, trying to ignore the first part of what he had said. "At least until they get to know me and learn differently. You of all people ought to know I don't need any more protection than I already have. Plus, years ago, you taught me self-defense."

More than anything else, she believed his phone call three months ago had simply been a knee-jerk re-action on his part, habit developed over the years. As for the rest of what he'd just said, she had no idea what to think about it.

She moved away from him and around her desk in an instinctively slow manner, almost as if she were walking away from a wild animal that she didn't want to startle into violence.

He followed her with his intense gaze. "Okay, so now that I've told you why Molinari enjoys being with you, tell me why in hell you enjoy being with him."

She sat down and immediately felt better with the desk between them. "You mean besides the fact that he's handsome, charming, and knows how to show a girl a good time? Gee, David, I don't know."

He went quiet and still. Watching him, she received the eerie sensation of a deadly jungle cat gathering its strength right before it was about to pounce. But in-stead he relaxed, subtly, muscle by muscle. If she hadn't been watching him so carefully, she would have missed the slow release of tension from his body.

She'd once heard one of her cousins say that David could move like lightning or stay perfectly still for hours at a time, but this was the first time she'd wit-nessed the extraordinary control he could hold over his body. "I think we'd better choose another subject, don't you?" she said mildly.

"You don't like that subject?" Taking in a deep,

cleansing breath, he slowly let it go, then slipped his hands into the pockets of his slacks and sent a casual glance around her flower-filled office. "Okay, then, why don't we talk about all these flowers? Since I'm sure you really aren't going into the flower business, it's got to be something else."

"They'll all be cleared out of here in a couple of hours," she said, her voice noncommittal.

"Including those stacked out in the hallway?"

She nodded, knowing all too well that his casual interest was a sham. He was baiting her, but she had no intention of giving him the satisfaction of rattling her any more than he already had. "Every few days I have them divided up and taken to nursing homes and hospitals."

"Which must mean that new flowers arrive every day, and which also must mean that you have a very ardent admirer."

He knew exactly who the flowers were from. She smiled at him. "You look good, David. I've never understood why, but your work obviously agrees with you."

His return smile held little humor. "Yet another change of subject, Kylie? We can't seem to agree on anything, can we? Not even a topic of conversation."

"I think we can both agree that once again you were lucky to make it home at all. How many scars do you have by now, anyway?"

"I'd be happy to take off my clothes if you want to count."

She was surprised. Being deliberately provocative with her was a radical departure from the way he'd always treated her. And there'd certainly been nothing subtle about the way he'd let her know he was angry with her over her meeting and friendship with Allesandro. Even so, his anger seemed far beyond the bounds of what she would have expected.

In a way, she supposed she could understand his reasoning. He lived in a world in which a good guy often turned out to be a bad guy, and a bad guy was as dangerous and unpredictable as a striking snake. But she couldn't understand his being provocative with her. It made her remember too many things she wanted to forget. She looked down at the papers on her desk, lifting one aside as if she needed to get back to work. He didn't take the hint.

"No? You don't want me to take off my clothes? Then what, Kylie?"

She laid the paper down while she searched for something neutral to say. "So how long are you home for this time? Is this one of your flying visits or will you be home for a while?"

"It depends."

"On what? Until the next world crisis erupts and they call on you to save the day?"

"You never know," he said, suddenly moving to take up his original position, one hip and thigh on the desk. "I may decide that the next crisis that needs my undivided attention is right here."

"You mean *me?*" she asked, shocked into laughter. "Save yourself the trouble, David. I know exactly what I'm doing."

"So then why is your family worried about you?"

"They aren't, and I don't believe they told you they

were." She paused, knowing she'd just lied, and by the look on his face, he knew it too. Damn it. She was going to have to work harder on guarding her expression. "Okay, maybe they are somewhat worried, but they haven't said much to me about it. They have enough confidence in me that they know I'll make the right decision."

"Maybe they do, but I don't." His fist came down on her desk. "What in the hell do you think you're doing, Kylie, fooling around with one of the most infamous men in America?"

She was beginning to enjoy herself. For once she felt she had the upper hand, because David didn't have a clue to what was going on between her and Allesandro. "Fooling around?"

"You know what I mean."

"I'm not sure I do. Let me get this straight. You think he's one of the most infamous men in America?" She shook her head, pretending to be baffled. "You know, I was positive it would be the world."

He leaned his body toward her until he was looming over her. "This isn't a joking matter. Molinari is the head of one of the largest crime families there is, and the very fact that he was able to wrest control of it away from his uncle means that he's deadly."

"*Really?* Thank you for that fascinating piece of information. I had no idea."

"*Kylie—*"

There was a knock at the door, it slowly opened, and a pale round face appeared around the corner. "Ms. Damaron?"

"My money says this is Clifford," David muttered with irritation and straightened away from her.

She swiveled her chair back to the desk. "Come in."

With a wary glance at David, her assistant walked quickly to her. "I'm sorry you had to wait for these, Ms. Damaron." He placed a thick leather folder squarely in front of her on her desk. "It won't happen again."

She opened the folder and quickly paged through its contents until she found what she wanted. She glanced up at the young man. "Thank you, Clifford. That's all for now."

"Yes, Ms. Damaron." With a nod and another wary glance at David, he did a race walk to the door and ever so quietly shut it behind him.

David cut his eyes to her. "*New*, I'm guessing?"

She nodded, leaning back in her chair again. "He's still getting his bearings and he's a little nervous."

"Where's Jack?" he asked, naming her head assistant. "Isn't he the one who usually trains your new people? I thought no one got this close to you without extensive training."

"Normally that's true. But I'm working with a skeleton staff this week so that Jack and the others can have this time off to be with their families for the holidays."

"Very nice. Now let's get back to Molinari, who thinks he can win you over by cleaning out every damn flower shop in New York City." He gave a disdainful thump to another one of her roses. An instant bruise appeared on the previously perfect petal.

She smiled, falsely sweet. "Give Allesandro a break,

David. He started out by showering me with diamonds."

He uttered a string of colorful and highly profane oaths.

She waited until he had finished. "I sent them back, of course." She paused. "David, if the sole reason you're here is to try to talk me into making a break from Allesandro, then you're wasting your time."

"I don't see it that way."

"Of course you don't, because that's the way *I* see it." She pulled the vase of roses out of his reach, reflecting that she was no longer having fun. Her nerves were beginning to wind into tight knots.

He slowly shook his head. "It seems we can't agree on anything."

"Did you really think we could?"

"We used to be able to."

"That was a long time ago."

"Funny. My recollection is that it wasn't so long ago. Seven years can go very fast."

She picked up a pen and tapped out a nervous beat against the desk. "I'm surprised. It would seem to me, given the life you lead, each day would seem like a thousand."

He exhaled. "Okay, Kylie, let's back away from yet another argument that's about to break out between us."

"I'm certainly willing." She put the pen down.

He nodded. "Okay—let's try this subject. One of the reasons I'm home is because it's only a few days until Christmas and as you know, the General always wants me home at this time of year."

David's father was a four-star general, recently re-tired, but they both knew the general to whom David was referring was his mother.

"Of course." She knew better than to think she would be important enough to bring David home all on her own.

"It's Christmastime, Kylie. Can you and I please try to have a little goodwill between us?"

"Goodwill?" she asked, her brows knitted with con-sternation. "If you're asking that we stop arguing, I'm all for it. Just don't try to tell me what to do and we'll be fine."

He pushed off from the desk and walked to the nearest window that looked out over New York City. Her office, along with the offices of her cousins, was on one of the highest floors of the Damaron Tower. The only floors higher held the family apartments. Al-though his back was to her, she could see he was watch-ing her reflection in the glass.

"I'm hoping that you and I can spend some time together during the holidays," he said slowly. "We have a lot of things to talk about."

"What things?" she asked, surprised and distrust-ful.

He glanced at her. "We can start with tonight. I'd like to take you out to dinner."

Her mouth nearly fell open. "Take me out? You mean like a date?"

"Why not?"

She was as stunned as if he'd asked her to jump off the top of the Tower. "I'm sorry, David, but I already have an engagement tonight."

He looked over at her. "With Molinari?"

"As a matter of fact, yes."

"Cancel it."

"I can't just cancel at the last minute, even if I wanted to—which I don't." She was actually relieved she had a previous engagement. The prospect of spending hours with David when she had no idea what he wanted from her was unthinkable. It had taken her a long time to put herself back together after the night of her twenty-first birthday. She never wanted to go through something like that again. "And by the way, you just told me what to do again."

He was silent for a moment. "My apologies." He continued to stare out the window as the clock on her desk clicked the seconds away. She couldn't imagine what was going on in his mind, but, she decided, she didn't really want to know. It was easier for her not to—and safer. Finally he turned back to her. "Are you staying in the city tonight?"

"I'll be staying here for the next few days, right up until Christmas Eve day. I have some business pending that needs my attention, plus I still have Christmas shopping to do."

"Then how about having dinner with me tomorrow night?"

"I'll have to see how tomorrow goes," she said, giving herself twenty-four hours to come up with an excuse.

He nodded. "Then I guess I'll be seeing you around." He strolled across her office in the same graceful way he had entered it. He opened the door, then looked back at her. "I also have business here in the city, and Wyatt offered me the use of his apartment, since he's already left for the country to spend some time with his new bride."

Wonderful, she reflected. Wyatt's apartment was right across the hall from hers. "Have you met Annie yet?"

"No. I only arrived late last night."

"Well, you'll like her. She's lovely and quite remarkable."

He smiled at her, the first genuine smile he'd given her since he'd invaded her office, a smile that she felt below her waist as a pool of warmth. "I'm sure I will."

"David?" she said, shocking herself with what she was about to say. "I truly am glad you made it home safely."

"Thank you." He stared at her for several moments, then left, quietly closing the door after him.

And immediately she felt empty.

Great, she thought, staring at the door where moments before David had stood. Just great. He'd just done two things he'd never done before. He'd asked her out on a date and he'd apologized to her.

Quite clearly, he was trying to break up the relationship she'd developed with Allesandro, perhaps by trying to get her interested in *him* again. But it would do him no good.

She was no longer a lovesick young woman and she was equal to any tactic he might come up with. He thought Allesandro was dangerous, but Allesandro had never once come close to hurting her as David had, nor did Allesandro present her with anywhere near the danger David did.

TWO

The linen, china, and flatware were of the finest. The wine was perfection. The music was lovely and unobtrusive. The food had been sublime, the service superb. And the man sitting across from her, Kylie reflected, was tall, slim, and elegant, with movie-star-handsome looks, olive skin, dark brown eyes, and brown hair lightly streaked with gray. He was also in love with her.

Unfortunately, she didn't, and couldn't, love him in return.

Three months ago, after Allesandro had given her the information Wyatt had needed, he'd asked her to stay for lunch. He had seemed so far removed from the stereotypical crime figure most people had in their minds that, out of curiosity, she'd accepted his invitation. But after she'd returned to New York, Allesandro had kept calling, going out of his way to get her to see him again.

At first she'd refused, but something she'd heard in

the family meeting the night before she'd flown to Wyoming kept coming back to her. That night, Jonah had phoned a contact in the Treasury Department and had returned to the meeting with some interesting information. According to Jonah's contact, Allesandro was smooth, cool, educated, and street-smart. In short, the contact had said, he was the Feds' worst nightmare, because so far they hadn't been able to lay a finger on him.

Once again her curiosity had been piqued. Why couldn't the Feds get anything on him? He was obviously extremely good at what he did, but the federal government had a prodigious amount of power. There had to be another reason.

Finally she'd accepted Allesandro's dinner invitation and had had a delightful evening. Other dinners had followed and trust had slowly built between the two of them until she'd finally received an answer to her question.

Little by little, so as not to attract too much attention, Allesandro was quietly making his family business legitimate.

She volunteered her help, though they both knew she couldn't become directly involved, nor could he reveal to her specific details about any of his unlawful activities. If he did, she could be legally jeopardized. So Allesandro would run theoretic business scenarios by her and she would give him the benefit of her knowledge.

She enjoyed their friendship and was more than happy to help him. She genuinely liked him and wanted legitimacy for him. Consequently it had taken her a while to realize that Allesandro had fallen in love with her. But now that she had, she'd reluctantly decided that this dinner had to be their last together.

Now, the meal had been cleared away, the waiters had disappeared, and they'd been left to their wine, the music, and their conversation.

"Have I told you that you look particularly beautiful tonight?"

She smiled. "One of the things I love about this restaurant is how flattering the candlelight is."

"The candlelight has nothing to do with it."

"Thank you." She was wearing the same slim black wool sheath that she'd worked in all day, the same one David had touched. When it had come time to leave for the restaurant, she'd simply added a diamond sunburst brooch and matching earrings that had been her mother's, and exchanged her pumps for black high heels with straps that crisscrossed over the top of her feet.

"You know, Allesandro, you didn't have to rent out the entire restaurant again tonight."

"I've told you before. I won't have your reputation ruined simply because you're gracious enough to accept a dinner invitation from me." His gaze and voice were soft as he looked at her.

With a smile, she absently swirled the wine in her glass. "My reputation can take it."

He shook his head. "Maybe, but it doesn't have to. We do it this way and no one has to see you with me. The chef, the help, and the musicians are either already on my payroll or have been paid enough that they won't say a word."

She'd become accustomed to such statements from him. In a very charming, Old World way, he was taking care of her, but in another very real way, the statement was chilling. She never asked what would happen to the person who might break the confidence and tell all to a news reporter, for instance. With Allesandro, she simply concentrated on the definite progress he was making to go completely legitimate.

In many ways, she was handling Allesandro's career the same way she had handled David's career for so many years. Don't ask. Don't interfere. The less she knew, the less she worried.

When she was younger, she could understand why her older cousins had kept the information they knew about David to themselves. But she was an adult now and her responsibilities equaled those of her cousins. She knew everything as soon as they did, except when it came to David. That wasn't their fault, however. It was her choice.

She'd convinced herself she didn't want to know, and the bits and pieces of information she did have regarding him came to her because of something she'd accidentally overheard or from an idle piece of conversation that started while the family was together for some event. But she never asked.

Of course there were times she couldn't avoid hearing about him, times when he would be brought up during a business meeting. Because of his work, David was often in the position to help the family, either by a carefully dropped piece of information or his presence in times when they needed his expertise to help watch their backs.

But her opinion still hadn't changed. She still didn't want to know about the dangerous assignments he was sent on, nor what menacing, darkly threatening routes he had to walk to accomplish his mission. He had a way of suddenly disappearing from her life, then just as suddenly reappearing, as he had this afternoon.

She couldn't depend on him. She couldn't trust him.

"Kylie," she heard Allesandro say. "Where did you go?"

She blinked, then smiled apologetically. "I'm sorry. I was thinking about a problem I have to deal with later, but I shouldn't have been thinking about it during our time together."

"I agree," he said with dry humor. "When you're with me, I want your mind only on me."

"Which you deserve."

"Thank you." A waiter approached bearing a large tray of exquisite desserts. Allesandro glanced at her. "What would you like to start off with?"

She couldn't help but laugh. "Start off with? I couldn't even eat *one*—although," she hastened to add for the waiter's benefit, "they all look delicious."

Allesandro gestured, and with a nod, the waiter disappeared.

The band segued into a hauntingly lovely tune, and for a moment she listened and considered what she was about to do. Allesandro had shown her nothing but kindness and respect. She'd give anything if she didn't have to cause him pain, but she couldn't let him go on loving her when she couldn't love him in return.

"Allesandro, I have something I need to tell you tonight."

With a wry smile on his face, he pushed back a little from the table and crossed his legs. "Why do I feel as if I'm not going to like this?"

"None of what I'm about to say is meant to hurt you. I want you to know that."

"Now I *know* I'm not going to like it." His eyes held sadness. "Is it the danger, Kylie? The danger that is still inherent in my life? The need to meet in empty restaurants and theaters? Is that what is bothering you?"

She shook her head. "It's none of those things. You forget there has always been a certain amount of inherent danger in my own life."

"I realize that, but your family is legitimate—on the side of angels, if you will—and mine is perceived as the exact opposite."

"Perceived? True. But someday soon you're going to be able to tell everyone that you're one hundred percent legitimate.

"Perception is everything, Kylie. And it is nothing. But for your help and suggestions, I'll always be grateful to you. You have a truly brilliant mind for business. I hope your family appreciates you."

She smiled. "They do, and I've been more than happy to help you, you know that."

He nodded. "Yes, but we've gotten off the subject. Right now you have something you wish to tell me."

"Yes, yes, I do." It seemed to her that even the soft shadows in the corners of the restaurant had suddenly taken on a somber cast. "Allesandro, I've thoroughly enjoyed your company and the friendship that has grown out of the time we've spent together these last three months, but now it's time for me to say good-bye."

Taking several moments, he rearranged the napkin on his lap. "Why?"

"Because I don't love you."

"It doesn't matter," he said, his voice and gaze gentle. "My love for you is enough for both of us." He sat forward, his expression earnest. "Kylie, I *can* make you happy. And who knows? One day you may be surprised to find that you've fallen in love with me."

"You would be very easy to fall in love with, Allesandro."

"But not for you?"

"I'm sorry."

"You sound very certain. Am I right to think there is someone else?"

It was odd that she hadn't anticipated his question. She hadn't even thought about it, really. But the moment she heard his question, a picture of David had flashed into her mind.

"I want to answer you as honestly as I can," she said slowly, taking her time to consider her words. "I suppose you could say that there is someone else. He's been in and out of my life for as long as I can remember. But do I love him?" She thought for a moment, then shook her head. "No. He's much too difficult to love."

"Too difficult for you?" He shook his head. "Never underestimate yourself, Kylie. I believe in you and your ability to do anything you want."

All the sadness in the world was in his eyes and voice. She'd hurt him when it was the last thing in the world she'd wanted to do. "Thank you for your faith in me, but Allesandro, this other person is not the reason for my decision that we shouldn't see each other anymore. I simply think you deserve someone who will love you as you should be loved and that person can't be me."

He reached across the table for her hand. "We've never lied to each other, Kylie, so I have no choice but to believe what you're saying to me. But I hate it. In fact I can't even express to you how *much* I hate it. If I thought I had even a fraction of a chance, I'd fight for you, but I can see in your eyes that I don't." He paused, glanced away, then looked back at her, his dark eyes moist. "But Kylie, if you ever need a friend—I don't care what the reason—please don't hesitate to call me. You have my number. You'll always be able to reach me."

She smiled. "Thank you, Allesandro. I do consider you my friend, and I make the same offer to you. Please, call me if you ever need me. I'll be there for you."

He stared at her for a moment, then, with his hand still holding hers, he stood and drew her from her seat. "Goodbye, my friend," he said and bent his head to kiss the back of her hand.

"Goodbye, Allesandro."

He released her hand, and waited by the table as he always did for her to leave the restaurant by the front door. As usual, he would leave by the back.

Sadness engulfed her as she made her way to the front of the restaurant, where the maître d' stood waiting for her with her coat in his hands. She quickly slipped into it, then exited the restaurant.

Allesandro had done nothing to deserve the pain he was now feeling, the pain she had left him with. Her impulse was to go back into the restaurant and try to comfort him until he didn't hurt anymore, but she honestly didn't know what to say to him that wouldn't make his pain worse. No, he deserved much more comfort and love than she could give him, and she sincerely hoped he would find it.

Preoccupied with her thoughts, she walked out onto the sidewalk of the quiet side street where her car and driver always waited and looked straight into a pair of glittering golden eyes.

"David?"

He leaned casually against a menacing machine of a black Porsche, his arms folded over his chest, one ankle crossed over the other. He wore a mahogany-colored leather jacket over brown slacks and a sweater, and he looked as sleek and menacing as his car.

Her car and driver were nowhere in sight.

David straightened and shot back his cuff to look at his watch. "Your dinner ended early. Hope you had a lover's quarrel." He opened the passenger-side door and, with a wave of his hand, indicated that she should get in.

She crossed the sidewalk to him. "What are you doing here? And where's Tim?" Tim was the Damarons' head of security and, without any discussion, had quietly taken on the task of personally driving her to and from her meetings with Allesandro.

"I sent him back to the Tower."

"You . . . ?" It took a millisecond for her temper to ignite. "Who gave you the right to do something like that?"

"No one, but Tim knew you'd be safe with me. Get in."

"Tim had no right. He's paid by me and my family, not by you." Strangely, there was a look of patience on David's face that she hadn't seen in a long time. But then that was the problem. It *had* been too long.

"Kylie—"

She gestured at him with her evening bag. "I don't know what you think you're doing, but . . ." Her evening bag slipped from her hand.

They both knelt at the same time to retrieve it. She grasped it first, but her arm brushed against his and his hand closed over hers. Startled, she looked up at him. Heat flamed in the depths of his eyes. She felt the same heat in her limbs and stomach. Mere inches separated their lips. She only had to lean forward . . .

No. She wasn't going to get caught in that trap again.

She started to rise. A loud bang startled her, then another, identical to the first. David's hand shot out to yank her back down, just as the glass in the back window shattered.

He dove into the car, swung his long legs over the gear shift, and dragged her in after him. "Keep down!"

Crouching sideways on the floorboard so that her head didn't show above the window, she reached back and quickly pulled her door shut. The steady burst of gunfire sounded as if it were getting closer. Bullets struck the car, nicked the padded dashboard, and tore apart the passenger-side headrest.

Sitting as low as possible, David started the car, jammed the accelerator to the floor, and they took off with a leap of speed that flung her sideways against the seat.

"Are you all right?" David snapped out without taking his eyes off the street.

"Yes." It had all taken place within a matter of seconds. She'd lost one shoe and her hose were shredded where her legs had scraped against something, perhaps as David had dragged her into the car. She had no idea where her purse was. But she was fine. And terrified.

"You weren't hit?" He straightened in the seat.

"No, were you?"

"No."

"Could you tell who was shooting at us?"

"No," he said, his voice tight as he continuously glanced in his rearview mirror. "And I didn't think it was a good idea to hang around and find out."

Not with her safety to consider, he wouldn't. She looked up at him. Shadows and light moved rapidly across his face as they wove in and out of traffic as fast as possible, considering they were in Manhattan. They careened around corners and, with the almost constant blare of the horn, sped through red lights. From what she could tell, he was taking a back way to Damaron Tower.

She'd never seen his face this hard before. His profile appeared chiseled out of granite, with angles sharp enough to cut. She knew that if it hadn't been for her, he would have stayed and fought it out with whoever had shot at him. But he had been programmed long ago to take care of her, even if he'd been the one who'd done the programming.

"Is anyone following us?" Kylie asked.

"There was a car, but . . ."

"What?"

"I don't see them now, but stay down until I can be sure I've lost them."

"Do you have any idea who could have been shooting at you?"

He spared her a quick glance. "The better question would be who would be shooting at *you*, sweetheart."

"*Me?*"

He took another corner, then reached into his jacket pocket and pulled out a small cell phone. "Call Tim and alert him to what's happened. Tell him we're about ten minutes away from the Tower, and to watch for us, because we'll be coming in fast."

She did exactly as he told her, relating the information to Tim without emotion. She'd been in too many crises either to argue with David or to break down on the phone with Tim.

As soon as she pushed the end button on the cell, David said, "Okay, I think it's safe for you to get up now."

Maneuvering herself into the bucket seat was easier said than done, but being as small as she was helped. She kicked off her remaining shoe, then, fastening the seat belt, she glanced at David. His concentration was intense. He was in complete control of himself and the car, all the while remaining aware of his surroundings. She also knew that he was aware of her, not as a man would be aware of a woman, as he was a few minutes ago, but as someone he would die to protect. Even after all that had happened between them she knew that.

"What did you mean about me being the target?"

He took his eyes off the street for only moments. "Because, Kylie, I'd been standing out there for thirty minutes and no one so much as said hello to me. Also, there's no one in New York who would be shooting at me. My enemies are in the Middle East, and before I left, I made sure all loose ends were tied up."

She was stunned into silence. Could it really be that someone wanted her dead? Who? Why? It didn't make any sense, but she didn't have too much time to sort through her feelings because they were nearing the Tower.

She saw Damaron guards posted on either side of the private entrance, their weapons in slings over their shoulders. As soon as the first guard saw David's car approach, he lifted his radio and spread the information. Instantly the two double-thick steel gates that protected the underground parking area slid open. Then, as they flashed through them, the guards dashed in behind them and the gates closed.

She was safe inside the womb of Damaron Tower and knew that nothing could hurt her now. So why, she wondered as she glanced at David's hard face, did she still feel in peril?

As soon as Kylie walked into her cream and gold penthouse apartment, the phone started ringing. She tossed her keys into the marble bowl on the hall table and went to answer it.

"Hello?"

"Kylie, are you all right?" Allesandro asked urgently.

She dropped down into the comfort of a heavily cushioned gold brocade chair and rubbed her forehead. "I'm fine. I wasn't hit, nor was . . . my driver."

"Thank *God*. As soon as I heard the shots, I ran out, but you were already gone."

"David got me out of there quickly."

"He must have lightning reflexes. I couldn't have been more than seconds behind you."

"Allesandro, do you have any idea who was doing the shooting?"

"No, but it's being checked out as we speak. Whoever they were, they also got away quickly."

"Could it have been one of your enemies who might have wanted to send some sort of message to you through killing me?" It was hard for her to believe she was even saying the words. She felt as if she'd walked out of the restaurant and into a nightmare. But if it were true, at least the shooting would have made some sort of sense to her.

"I honestly don't know right now, but if you want an educated guess, I'd have to say no. There are people who would be extremely unhappy at the moves I'm making toward legitimacy. There is an old guard who strongly believe that the old ways are the best ways, and to do or think any other way is traitorous. Then there is the new guard. They would be unhappy because legitimacy will directly affect their incomes.

However, so far I've managed to keep a pretty tight lid on things."

Allesandro felt he had a tight lid on his business. David had said he'd tied up all his loose ends. They were both in control of their lives. Before tonight she had felt the same way. One of them was wrong and all the arrows were pointing straight at her.

"It only takes one person," she murmured.

"Which is exactly why I'm conducting a very thorough investigation. Believe me, Kylie. If it was an enemy of mine who tried to kill you—or a friend—I will not rest until I find him."

"Thank you. Please call me if you find out something."

"You can be sure I will. Oh, one more thing. I have your purse and shoe. They'll be messengered to you tomorrow."

"Thank you."

Her doorbell rang and she pushed herself up from the chair. "Allesandro, I have to go now."

"That's fine. Now that I know you're all right, I can turn my full attention to the problem at hand. I'll call you tomorrow."

"Good. I'll talk to you then."

She hung up the phone and went to open the door to a parade of her cousins, needing to see for themselves that she was all right. David brought up the rear.

She wasn't surprised that her cousins had all been informed. It was standard operating procedure. If a Damaron came under attack anywhere in the world, the rest were notified as soon as possible, because if one

Damaron was attacked, it could mean that the rest were also in danger.

Their precautions might seem over the top to some, but an entire generation of Damarons—their parents—had been wiped out with a single bomb planted in their plane, and their generation was determined that nothing like that would ever happen to them again.

"Are you okay?" Sin asked, and when she nodded, he immediately hugged her.

She wasn't really okay. She could feel reaction setting in—her knees had suddenly gone weak and tremors were starting to shake her body—but each of her cousins had to ask her the same question as Sin had and give her a hug. By the time she'd received her last hug, David was there, holding out a crystal snifter of brandy to her.

It didn't surprise her. David had always had a way of knowing how she felt and what she needed—he had, at least, until it came to matters of the heart.

"Thank you," she murmured and sank onto the sofa. Her cousins arrayed themselves around her.

Beside her, Sin took her hand. "Kylie, as soon as Tim deployed his men, he notified us. Honey," he said, his tone unusually careful, "I'm afraid the way it looks right now, Molinari was responsible for the attack on you."

She'd known that the first person her family would think of would be Allesandro and she didn't blame them. Allesandro was the obvious choice, but then they didn't know him as she did. "The attack didn't come from him—I know that as well as I know my name. In fact, he's already called to find out if I was all right."

"I didn't mean to imply the attack came from him personally. But in one way or another, he has to be the cause."

She met Sin's gaze levelly. "If that's true, he will find out. He's already begun his own investigation and will let me know either way as soon as possible."

"Are you sure you didn't do something tonight to upset the man?" David drawled from his position across the room, his elbow resting on the mantel of the marble fireplace.

She *had* done something to upset Allesandro tonight, but since she knew he would never have done such a thing no matter what she did, she ignored David and addressed her cousins. "Is there something going on with our business that I don't know about? Something that's happened within the last three or four hours, for instance?

In unison, her cousins shook their heads.

The question had been a long shot on her part. No Damaron cousin was ever left out of the loop, no matter where they were or how old they were.

From the very first meeting they'd held after their parents' deaths, her older cousins had included her. At the time she'd only been five, but she'd sat at the big conference table and colored in her coloring book while they—as incredibly young as they had been—had drawn up the blueprint and set into motion the Damaron International that existed today. By the time she'd turned thirteen, it had suddenly occurred to her that she understood most of what they were saying.

And what she didn't understand, they would patiently explain until she did.

"On the other hand," Jonah said, with a look at Sin that she easily interpreted as meaning to back off of Allesandro for now, "we all are aware that we have enemies we don't even know about and we've already started our own investigation. But until we find out who took those shots at you, Kylie, security will remain at its highest."

She absently nodded, understanding that they didn't want to upset her tonight any more than was necessary. Tomorrow would probably be a different matter, but tonight they were handling her with kid gloves.

She sipped her brandy, while her mind raced back over the business dealings she'd conducted during the past year. There'd been no threats made against her, written or otherwise, or she would have been informed. And no matter how hard she thought, she couldn't come up with anyone who might want her dead.

Unfortunately, though, as Jonah had implied, there were a lot of sick people in the world, and she knew that for some, her last name was enough to want her dead.

"If you think of anything, let us know," Lion said to her. "In the meantime, you look exhausted. We'll go and let you get some rest."

As they all stood, Jonah looked at her. "Do you plan to leave the Tower tomorrow?"

Kylie shook her head. "I don't have any definite plans, but I still have some Christmas shopping to do."

"I think we all do," Sin said. "And speaking for

myself, I've exhausted the catalogues and personal shoppers. Now I'm down to my family list; I need to get out and see what the stores are offering to make my selections."

"Same with me," Jonah said. "No one is going to choose my son's electric train set but me."

Sin nodded. "My thought exactly."

Agreement murmured from everyone.

"Maybe we can get a few stores to open up after hours for us so that we don't have to worry too much about security," Lion said. "I'll have one of my assistants handle that and get back to you all."

"That will be great. Thanks, everyone." She rose and began to walk her cousins to the door. "I know Joanna will be safe with Cale, but what about the others?"

"Tim's on it," Sin said. "Everyone's well guarded."

"Good, but what about Yasmine? She's all the way down in Texas."

"Same thing," Jonah said. "She didn't have guards on her before, but now she does."

"Do we know these guards? Can we trust them?" Kylie asked.

Lion walked to her and took her hands in his. "We wouldn't have hired them if we didn't think we could, baby. Plus, as we speak, a team of our own men is in the air, heading down there to take over. In fact, they're probably only a couple of hours away by now."

"A lot can happen in a couple of hours," she murmured. Over the years she'd tried very hard to keep her anxieties about her cousins' safety to herself, and most of the time she succeeded. But tonight she hadn't been able to. As much as they all traveled, she never felt completely worry-free about her cousins unless they were all at home.

She'd never been afraid for herself, but rather for everyone else she loved. And now was no exception, even when she knew that *she'd* been the target.

She'd learned at an early age how fickle life could be and how in the blink of an eye someone you loved could be taken away from you. Consequently, in the deepest, darkest part of her psyche, she had a terrifying fear of losing someone else she loved to a sudden, senseless tragedy.

She glanced around the room and saw nothing but understanding. She'd once overheard her cousins talking about her, saying that, of all of them, she'd been the most damaged by that long-ago plane crash. Only when she'd become an adult had she fully understood how much damage that plane crash had done to her.

Lion smiled down at her. "And before you ask, Nathan is still in Brussels and is also being well guarded, right along with the others who are still out of the country."

She nodded. "I just wish everyone was here together, that's all."

Lion kissed her forehead. "Don't worry, baby. We're all going to be safe."

"Right." If there'd been less than full confidence in her voice, no one said anything, and as each of her cousins left, they kissed and hugged her and murmured words of reassurance.

With a sigh, she shut the door behind them and locked it, even though she knew that tonight there would be a guard on her door, plus another team of guards for the floor and elevators. Tonight even a mouse would have trouble going undetected if it tried to make its way up to the top floors of the Tower.

She made her way slowly back into the living room and stopped. David was still there, reclining in the gold brocade chair, framed by the Manhattan lights that shone beyond her apartment's wall of windows.

An exotic, elegant savage she'd once considered hers.

THREE

"What are you still doing here?" Her tone was almost monotone, Kylie realized. She felt spent, with no energy left for any emotions.

"I wanted to make sure you're all right."

"I am, thank you. In fact, I'm going to take a shower right now and get ready for bed."

David nodded his head approvingly. "Then I'll wait until you get out."

"Why?" she asked, able to summon only mild curiosity.

He shrugged. "I'm not tired. I'm only a few steps away from where I'm going to sleep tonight. And I want to make *really* sure that you're all right before I go."

"I'm fine, but if you want to stay for a little bit longer, then do it."

She lingered in the shower, leaning against the wall and allowing the warm water to flow over her, while the events of the evening played over and over in her head. She still couldn't get the hurt in Allesandro's eyes out of her mind when she'd told him she would never love him. But another, stronger image overlaid that one, an image of her bending down to pick up her purse just as the bullets began to fly over her head. If she hadn't dropped her purse, if she hadn't bent to get it, if David hadn't reacted so quickly . . . And worse yet, no one knew a thing about who would want her dead.

Eventually, though, she had to convince herself that there was no use turning herself inside out, trying to figure this out. For tonight, at least, she had to let it go so that she could sleep. She was going to need a clear mind in the morning. She knew that everything possible was being done to track down whoever was responsible. For now, it had to be enough for her.

After the shower, she slipped into her favorite cream silk nightgown that was fleeced on the inside, then put on her beige cashmere robe and soft, fuzzy slippers—her *comfort* night clothes.

Back in the living room she found David exactly where she'd left him, except that he was now talking on the phone. But the moment he saw her, he murmured a few quick words and hung up.

She didn't have to ask why he'd been using her phone, because she knew he'd been reaching out to his own contacts. By this time tomorrow, countless people would have been touched by what had happened tonight.

Tired, but still too keyed up to try to go to sleep, she sank down onto the sofa and pulled her slippered feet up under her. A log, she noticed, burned cheerfully in the fireplace. "Thanks for starting the fire."

"No problem." He studied her for several moments. "Would you like some more brandy?"

"Please." She watched as he rose and moved gracefully across the room to her bar, usually concealed by a paneled wall. Earlier, when he'd first filled her glass, he'd known exactly where to press to reveal the bar.

After all these years, he knew so much about her and her life. He'd been the first to notice that she was having a reaction to what had happened. Her saving grace, she supposed, was that he knew nothing about what was going on inside her mind.

Crossing back to her, he turned off several lights. Until then, she hadn't realized that the lights had started to bother her eyes. "Thank you," she murmured, reaching for the snifter he held out to her.

"You're welcome." His own brandy in his hand, he dropped down on the sofa, a cushion away from her.

She nodded toward the wall of glass behind him. "Look, it's snowing."

He glanced over his shoulder. "So it is."

"I hope it snows for Aunt Abigail's Christmas Eve party," she said, her voice barely above a whisper. "Light, beautiful flakes that will give us a fresh coat of snow for Christmas morning."

"Somehow it always does," he said quietly. "Abigail wants a snowfall for her party and she always gets it. It used to puzzle me until I figured out that not even Mother Nature is impervious to your great-aunt's charm.

Kylie smiled.

"It's nice to see you smile again," he said, his voice low and slightly husky.

She sipped at her brandy. "It's good to feel like smiling."

"No one is going to harm you, Kylie. Or any of your family. I don't want you worrying about that. We'll find out who it was."

"I know."

He shifted his body around so that he was facing her, his knee resting on the cushion between them, his arm along the back of the couch, his hand close enough to touch her. "Kylie, I need to ask you a question, but I don't want to upset you or make you angry."

"Then don't ask the question." She took a sip of her brandy.

"I have to, because you're the only one who knows the answer." He paused, searching her face. She wasn't sure what he was looking for and couldn't find the strength to care.

"You said that Molinari was not responsible for the shooting."

"That's right." If she'd given any thought at all to the matter, she would have known David would bring up the subject of Allesandro again. But the brandy was relaxing her. She didn't want to think or to argue.

"You also said you'd already talked to him. Did you *ask* him if he was responsible?"

"No, David," she said softly, wearily, "I didn't. Allesandro would no more have someone try to kill me than he would have someone try to kill himself."

"Maybe he wasn't trying to kill you. Maybe he was just trying to frighten you."

"And the purpose of frightening me would be *what* exactly?"

"You tell me. Is he trying to get you to do something you don't want to do? Something about your relationship, for instance? If you two aren't already . . . close, he could be pushing for that. Or even marriage."

She didn't miss the edge that had sliced through his voice when he'd hinted at her and Allesandro being lovers.

"Please, just drop the subject. I know it wasn't Allesandro as well as I know it wasn't you."

"You're *that* certain?"

"Yes, I am."

He was silent for several moments, studying her. But it was all right, because she couldn't feel the effects of the intensity on her skin as she usually could. It was as if the feeling parts of her had shut down to protect her.

She looked past him to the snow falling past her window. It was so lovely and peaceful and many times more preferable to focus on than him.

"Do you love him, Kylie?"

"It's really none of your business, David," she murmured. "Or anyone else's, for that matter."

"Those bullets came as close to hitting me as they did to you, Kylie. I think that gives me a few rights."

Her numbed state received a harsh jolt. She supposed he was right.

The bullets that were fired at her tonight *had* changed certain things: Her belief that she needed to worry about the others in her family, but never herself. Her wish to keep private what was between her and

Allesandro. Lastly, and perhaps more importantly, what she now owed David. After all, he'd saved her life.

She looked back to him, her brow knitted with her thoughts. "Those bullets had nothing to do with Allesandro, nor anything to do with what's between Allesandro and me."

"Then convince me of that."

"You already have your mind made up about him. Nothing I can say will convince you differently."

"Try me."

She drew in a deep breath, then slowly exhaled. David deserved to know a couple of things, she decided, but certainly not everything. He didn't need to know Allesandro's bid for legitimacy, for instance.

"Okay. As you obviously already know, Allesandro started pursuing me after we met in Wyoming. Since most of the time he works here in New York, as do I, it was easy for us to go out to dinner once we both got back here. With me, he's always been funny and kind and considerate, and I enjoyed his company immensely. But something happened that I didn't expect. He fell in love with me."

"I'm not surprised."

His comment drew her gaze from the window to him. "That he fell in love with me?"

"No," David said softly. "That you didn't expect him to."

His statement made her pause, but in the end, she decided she wasn't up to deciphering it. "Well, unfortunately, I can't love him back and, much as I hated causing him pain, I felt I had to tell him."

"You told him tonight?"

"Yes, I told him it was time we said goodbye."

"And how did he take it?"

"Like the perfect gentleman he's always been with me. There's no question he was hurt, but somewhere inside him, I think he already knew." She shook her head as she remembered. "I *hated* having to hurt him like that, but it had to be done, and we parted friends."

"I see," David said thoughtfully. "Thank you for telling me, Kylie. Now I can stop focusing on Molinari as being directly responsible. However, that doesn't rule out his enemies."

"I told you. He's checking on that." She rubbed her forehead.

A frown crossed David's strong-boned face. "Do you have a headache?"

"No. It's just that a lot has happened tonight, and I'm not doing a very good job of dealing with it."

"That's only natural."

"Not for you."

"It's caught me off guard too, Kylie."

"Not in the same way." She paused. "I'm sorry—I haven't even said thank you yet."

"Thank you for what?"

"For saving my life. If it hadn't been for you, I would have stood up. I had no idea what the sound was—a car backfiring, maybe. But never in a million years would I have guessed bullets were being fired at me. You might have been caught off guard, David, but your reaction was instantaneous."

He shrugged his broad shoulders. "It's my training. But even if I hadn't been there, Tim would have been, and you wouldn't have been standing out in the open

arguing with me. You would have come out of the restaurant and immediately climbed into the car as you're
accustomed to doing, and Tim would have gotten you
away safely."

"Well, he wasn't there and you were, so it's *you* I
have to thank. So thank you very much."

He didn't reply, though he continued to gaze at
her. The intensity in his eyes had vanished, she saw
with some surprise. Now there was only softness, a
softness she recognized all too well. It was the way he
used to look at her and over the years it had meant
many things—protection, friendship, love. But tonight
she couldn't begin to decipher it, and because she
couldn't, she felt a bit uneasy.

Finally, he said, "You're entirely welcome. And now
it's my turn to say I'm sorry."

"For what?"

"For a couple of things. I should have known better
than to let you stand there arguing with me, without
first insisting that you get into the car."

"I was the one who started the argument. It was my
fault."

"But as I said, I should have known better. I should
have insisted, even if it meant picking you up bodily
and putting you in the car myself."

"We're talking about seconds, David."

"No, Kylie. We're talking about life and death. If
you hadn't dropped your purse—"

"But I did. Quit beating yourself up about what you
didn't do. The fact is, thanks to your quick thinking,
we're both alive."

"Right—we are." He paused for several seconds,

his gaze even softer. "There's also another reason that I'm sorry about what happened."

"What's that?"

"I'm sorry you had to learn what it's like to be shot at."

He was right, she reflected. She'd learned a lot of things in her life, but before tonight, she hadn't known what it was like to have a bullet fired at her. "You've known for years what it's like."

"Yes."

"Is it something you ever get used to?"

"No, not really."

"It was awful."

"I know. I know."

He ran the back of his hand down the side of her cheek. More warmth entered her bloodstream, and amazingly she no longer felt uneasy. It was as if their shared experience earlier that night had broken down at least a few of the barriers they'd erected over the years and had sent them back to another time when just being with him made her feel better and they could talk easily with one another. It wouldn't last, she told herself, but while it did, she should accept it, especially now when her raw nerves badly needed soothing.

"But you know, Kylie," he said, his voice and touch still soft as he allowed his hand to drop onto her shoulder, intimate and comforting, "you were marvelous. You kept your head and did everything I told you to do."

Her lips, curved slightly into a half-smile. "That's *my* training."

"I know, but in a perfect world where everything is

good and right, you wouldn't need to have such training."

"I don't know a world like that, do you?"

"No, unfortunately, I don't. But I've fought in hell-holes all over the globe trying to make sure that none of the evil elsewhere reaches where you live." Abruptly, he pulled his hand away from her shoulder as if he'd said something he regretted. "Never mind. You're tired right now, but tomorrow you'll feel better."

"Tomorrow there'll still be someone out there who wants me dead."

"Maybe, but he won't have a chance in hell of getting you because you'll be too well guarded."

She shook her head in amazement. "To you this is all so commonplace, a day at the office. But as much as I've been trained to know exactly what to do in situations such as the one that happened tonight, I don't think it will ever become commonplace for me."

"Someone wanting you dead is not at all commonplace to me, Kylie," he said, his tone suddenly hard. "But investigations are already being conducted on several different levels. The best thing you can do right now is get a good night's sleep."

"I can't sleep yet."

"Then I'll stay with you until you can."

She looked at him. After all the years and all the anger, after all the pain and all the sadness, it should seem strange to be sitting with him, alone, in the middle of the night, but it didn't. Not tonight.

For a long time now she'd considered him her adversary. More than likely she would again. But tonight he was the David of old who had always been her ally, and memories came flooding back.

She slowly smiled. "This reminds me of the first night I spent at Abigail's. Do you remember?"

"Your first night?" He thought for several moments, then nodded. "Yes, of course. Your parents had been killed, and the memorial service had taken place that day."

She nodded. "I was only five and Jo was fifteen. The boys were a little older. Yasmine was able to stay at home with Lion and their maternal grandmother, but it was decided that Jo and I would live with Abigail until we finished school."

"Right. And I was also staying there, because Dad was stationed in Europe and he and Mom wanted me to finish my schooling in America."

"It was all so frightening to me," she said softly. "I was used to my parents' trips. Beforehand, they always told me where they were going and showed me on a map. They also made me a special calendar so that I could see exactly when they would be back. They even left little notes for me to find that said they loved me." She paused. "You know, my mother hadn't originally planned to go on the trip."

"I'm not sure I knew that."

"Daddy kissed me goodnight the night before and as always had made me a calendar, but I expected Mother to be there when I woke up the next morning." She looked away toward the snow. "Apparently she made a last-minute decision to go with Daddy. I'll never really know why. Instead of waking me to tell me, she left me a note. When I woke up the next morn-

ing and found out she was gone, I was scared until Jo
helped me read the note." Her voice lowered to almost
a whisper. "It said that they loved me and would be
back in four days."

She felt tears well in her eyes, but she was able to
blink them quickly away. "So when Abigail appeared at
our house to tell us our parents wouldn't be coming
back home, I didn't understand it. I had a calendar that
clearly showed they'd be back in four days. I even had a
note that said the same thing. But four days later, Jo
and I had to move out of our own house and into Abigail's, which confused and frightened me even more."

He lifted his hand and lightly ran it over her hair.
"I'm afraid that in those first few days you were somewhat overlooked, though certainly not deliberately. It
was just that you were the smallest and the quietest,
and everyone else was so busy."

"I understand now. Sin, Jonah, and the others were
only kids themselves, but overnight they had to grow
up and make critical decisions."

He looked at her and smiled. "And that first night,
with Abigail trying to coordinate everything, along
with calling everyone to check on them, you got lost in
the shuffle."

She nodded, able to smile slightly at the memory.
"She'd never had children so she really didn't know
what to expect. But she did her best. She gave Joanna
and me separate bedrooms. Most of our belongings
had been transferred to them so that we would have
familiar things. She even took the time to tuck me into
bed that night. I was exhausted, but after she left, I was

too frightened to close my eyes. To make matters worse, a storm broke, so I went looking for Joanna."

The memory gentled his voice. "But you didn't know where she was and I just happened to have the bedroom across from yours."

She looked at him, caught up in the memory. "I could see a light beneath your door, so that's where I headed."

"I was up studying." He smiled. "I heard my door open and turned around to see you standing there, a little girl in a long, ruffled nightgown, holding a ragged teddy bear in one arm and a tattered blanket in the other. You were crying, but you weren't making a sound. I'd never seen anyone cry without making a sound."

"You opened your arms and said, 'Come here, baby,' and I ran right to you."

He shrugged. "What else could I do?

"There were a lot of other things you could have done," she said softly, "the main thing being to call Abigail. Any other fifteen-year-old boy would have. Instead you hugged me and let me cry." Her smile turned wry. "Your shirt was probably drenched by the time I got through."

He reached over and touched her cheek again. "You were just a sweet baby girl who was afraid and hurting. All you needed was someone to hold you and tell you everything was going to be all right."

"Which you did."

"Of course. You were a fairy child with an unbearable pain in your heart. I couldn't send you away."

Even as a boy, David had been big and fierce-looking, she reflected, but it had never once occurred to her to be afraid of him. Without a thought, she'd run straight into his arms. Even now, she was somewhat amazed at that. "You even told me I could stay with you for the night."

"There was no way I could let you go back to your room where you'd be all alone again. I was afraid you'd wake in the night and become scared all over again when you found yourself alone and in a strange room. Besides, the solution was so easy. I held you until you stopped crying, then tucked you into my bed, and you fell asleep, still holding your blanket and teddy bear.

"As I recall, I did wake up at least once."

"Twice, actually, but not for long. As soon as you saw me there beside you, you went right back to sleep."

"You couldn't have gotten much rest that night."

"I didn't mind, and after that night, Abigail and I figured out what to do so that you wouldn't be afraid anymore."

She nodded. "You kept your door open every night so that I could see you studying as I was falling asleep."

He smiled gently. "Worked like a charm."

"Except for those nights when the nightmares came. But even then you knew how to comfort me. You always woke up when you heard me crying, and you'd come across the hall, lay down on top of my covers, and hold me until I went back to sleep again."

"Like I said, you were just a little girl and you didn't know what to do with all the pain you were feeling."

"Except to run to you."

"Except to run to me," he agreed softly.

Looking back on that first night, she had no idea why she'd so instantly trusted him, but she had, and a part of her couldn't help but wish that the solution to her adult fears were that simple. She almost wished that tonight she could once more seek shelter within his arms and hear him tell her that everything was going to be all right. But it was impossible.

At least, though, for this brief period, they'd been able to talk to each other without arguing. It had been a long time since they'd been able to do that, and she didn't know how much she'd missed or needed it until this moment.

He moved his hand and allowed his fingers to tangle in her hair. "Back then your hair was the very same color as it is now and just as fine." He angled his head to look at her. "But happily I don't think you're as upset now as you were then."

"I've grown up."

"I think we covered that subject earlier this afternoon." His voice was suddenly husky and his gaze touched her lips.

Before she knew what was happening, he was kissing her. Just like that. As if he had every reason and right in the world to do so. And not small kisses of comfort on her cheek and eyes as he used to do when she was younger, but deep kisses, filled with longing and desire. The very suddenness and unexpectedness of it all prevented her from putting up any sort of guard against him, and seven years of estrangement dissolved in an instant.

Everything about him was so familiar. His hard mouth, his skillful lips—she remembered and responded to it all. He tasted of brandy, fire, and danger, even more danger than she'd felt earlier tonight when they were being shot at. But she was unable to do anything but return his kisses with an ever-increasing fervor. She hadn't felt this way in so long, as if there were nothing in the world more important than this moment. His darkly erotic scent was like an aphrodisiac to her, making her weaker until she was clinging to him, making her stronger until she was wordlessly demanding more.

Her hand slipped along his shoulder to the back of his neck. Then, sliding off the band that held his hair, her fingers glided upward to bring his lips down on hers harder. It worked. Thank God, it worked. He thrust his tongue, reaching deep into her mouth until she moaned with satisfaction. Heat gathered in all parts of her, burning away her bad memories, liquefying her bones and her resolve.

She almost cried out when, slowly, he broke off the kiss, pulling his mouth from hers and easing away from her. She searched his eyes for answers as to why he'd kissed her and how he felt, but she found nothing, not even satisfaction at making her feel the same, heated, passionate way she'd felt seven years ago. He didn't even seem to be breathing hard.

"If you get scared tonight," he said evenly, "or if you wake up and can't go back to sleep, or for any other reason, for that matter, remember that I'm right across the hall." In the first show of emotion since the kiss, his lips curved slightly. "I'll leave my door open."

"That won't be necessary." It wouldn't matter if he locked his door or left it wide open. Those days were gone. Besides, his kisses had left her too shaken and uncertain. To go to him tonight for any reason would be disastrous for her. "I doubt that I'll get scared, and actually I think I can sleep now." She rose and slowly made her way around the room, closing the bar, straightening already straight pillows, hoping he would get the hint and leave before she had to ask him to.

After watching her for several moments, he pushed himself up from the sofa. "Then I guess it's goodnight."

"Goodnight."

"Kylie?"

She turned around and looked at him. "What?"

"I was serious. If something frightens you, or you just can't sleep, call me and I'll come right over. Or just walk across the hall."

"Thank you." They both knew she wouldn't, she thought. They both knew that the innocent past they'd talked of tonight was a time they could never again recapture.

She'd once adored David and had trusted him with all her little secrets and fears. That unqualified adoration had lasted until she'd turned sixteen and developed an outsized crush on him. She liked to think she'd hidden her crush well, but knowing David as she did back then, she very much doubted it. She stopped telling him her secrets and he began to treat her with casual friendship and affection. Still, things had been simple between them. She just wished they had remained so.

He was almost to the door when she remembered something. "David?"

He turned around. "Yes?"

"You never said why you came to pick me up at the restaurant."

He looked at her for a moment, then smiled. "No, I didn't, did I? Sweet dreams."

FOUR

David stood in Kylie's office, staring blindly out the window. He was aware of the time only because the dark sky had begun to gently lighten to gray, a sign that the night was gradually releasing its hold and allowing the first hint of the day to reveal itself.

Kylie's snow was no longer falling.

Kylie . . .

Last night's shooting at the restaurant had shocked her, as it would any normal person. It had also left her unbalanced and consequently more accessible than she'd been in a long time. Her guard had dropped and that hadn't happened since the night she'd turned twenty-one, a night that was indelibly burned into his soul.

Abigail had thrown an extravaganza of a party to celebrate both Kylie's birthday and graduation from college. A large dance floor had been laid over the lawn and small white lights encircled every branch of every tree. Tables had been placed around the perimeter of the dance floor and were covered with fine white linens, and at the center of each were creamy gardenias and pale pink roses surrounding a tall white candle.

The society orchestra Abigail had hired had played a variety of songs, from the latest pop music to old standards, all chosen by Kylie. Likewise she'd chosen each item of the sumptuous buffet dinner. Family and friends had flocked in from all over the States and the world.

And Kylie . . .

Kylie had been dazzlingly beautiful. She'd worn a long blue silk strapless gown. The blue of the gown exactly matched the color of her eyes, and the bodice had been fashioned out of intricate pleats and tucks that swirled over her breasts and down to her waist. Her sister, Joanna, had created it for her, but Kylie had given the gown life. Just by wearing it, Kylie had transformed the garment into a shimmering, sensual vision.

A delicate strand of diamonds that had been her mother's glittered at her neck along with more diamonds at her ears, and with her every movement, the lightness of the long silk skirt had alternately billowed out around her or flattened against the curving lines of her lower body as she'd greeted her guests, laughed, drank champagne, and danced the night away, entrancing everyone who watched her.

Leaning against a pillar in the shadows of Abigail's back terrace, he'd followed Kylie's every move with a brooding gaze, and for the very first time since he'd known her, he allowed himself the luxury of being entranced as well.

He'd been aware of the crush she'd developed on him a few years earlier. She'd been lovely even then, graceful as a swan and fragile as a piece of fine crystal. But at that time he'd figured her crush would fade and he'd still regarded her as a kid sister, someone to tease and to protect.

But after she'd gone to college, things began to change and she suddenly seemed to blossom. She went from being lovely to breathtakingly beautiful. She also became aware of the effect she had on the young men who flocked around her. To her credit, though, she handled her newfound power over men well. She went out only in crowds of people her own age and rarely dated. That at least gave him some peace of mind.

Still, right before his eyes, Kylie was becoming a woman, with all the accompanying longings and emotions. He could see it in her body in the way she moved, and in the expression in her eyes when he sometimes caught her off guard. But all in all she was handling her ascent into womanhood much better than he. For him, it was hell.

Each time he saw her, heat stirred and grew in him until the need he felt for her began to claw at his insides.

He'd told himself she was too young. He'd told himself that if he acted upon the feelings he felt for her, he would be breaking a trust—not only the trust she had for him, but the trust of her entire family. As a result, he maintained a strong hold on his emotions whenever she was around him and he did his best to keep his relationship with her as it had always been.

Luckily, he wasn't often home, because by then he'd been deep into covert missions.

Still, there had been a couple of times when he'd been on a break from work and the Damarons had been in a crisis situation and had asked him for help, as they had the time they were trying to lure Steffan Wythe out of his Middle East compound. Their bait had been Wythe's stepdaughter, Jillian, whom Sin had kidnapped. Quite naturally the Damarons had been afraid that Wythe would strike back by kidnapping one of them.

At the time Kylie had been in college, so in order that she wouldn't miss any classes, he'd flown to her side. At night he'd slept on the couch in her off-campus apartment and during the day he had waited for her outside her classrooms. Night or day, it had been hellishly hard on him.

It had seemed to him that every man on campus wanted Kylie. That thought alone had driven him half crazy, because he knew all too well what it was to want her. More than that, though, he couldn't stand the thought of someone else having her.

For the first time, he considered his friendship with the Damarons a curse. As much as he wanted Kylie, he was there to protect her as he had for most of her life, not seduce her.

But that knowledge didn't stop the wanting, the craving, the needing. Only his determination and dedication to keep her safe had saved him.

But on the night of her birthday party, as practically every young man lined up to dance with her, he'd known he wasn't going to be able to ignore what he felt for her much longer. Watching her go laughingly into the arms of one man after another was tearing him apart inside.

By midnight the party was still going strong, but for the moment, at any rate, the music had slowed and become more romantic. When he saw yet another man step up to Kylie, he turned away. He had to leave, he reflected, or quite simply he was going to kill the next man he saw putting his hands on her.

The Damarons were accustomed to the demands of his job, and there was no need to offer an explanation for his departure. As for the rest of the guests, they didn't even know he was there.

He started toward the house just as Kylie materialized before him with a whisper of silk.

"You can't leave now, David," she said lightheartedly.

"Why not?" He'd arrived at the party late, so this was the first time all evening that he'd been close to her.

Even in the shadows of the terrace, the diamonds around her neck and at her ears sparkled on her skin. "Because you haven't danced with me yet."

"You don't need to dance with me. You have more than enough partners."

"But they're not you."

The heat that stirred in his veins hardened his voice. "Does it matter?"

She looked up at him through the thickness of her lashes. "Very much. You know how important you are to me."

He knew. He was important to her as a protector, a

confidant, a friend. She had no idea how often he thought of her and imagined how it would be to take her, to make her his, until his blood cooled and his appetite for her was sated.

"How did you even know I was up here?" he asked gruffly. As closely as he'd watched her, he'd never once seen her look his way.

"I just knew."

"Did you also know that I was just about to leave?"

She nodded. "Yes."

No. He didn't want to think that she'd been watching him. He didn't want to think that she cared one way or the other if he left without dancing with her. He especially didn't want to think there was something new in the way she was looking at him. But there was.

"Anyway," she said, "does it really matter?"

Yes, it did, he thought angrily. There was no way she could be that attuned to him without him knowing it.

She reached out and rested her hand lightly on his arm. "I want to have at least one dance with you before you leave, David. Abigail told me that tonight all of my wishes would be fulfilled."

"Somehow I think she was talking about the decorations and music."

"Maybe. Maybe not." With a laugh, she tugged on his arm. "Come on, David—dance with me. Please? You haven't even wished me a happy birthday yet."

"Happy birthday, Kylie." His tone was dark and rough, but it didn't deter her. It never had.

"Thank you. Now will you please dance with me? Call it your birthday present to me."

He stared at her for a moment, watching as the breeze lightly stirred through her gleaming hair, then moved across her skin caressingly, filling up his senses with its gardenia and rose scent. "All right, I'll dance with you. But not on the dance floor."

"Then where?"

"Here."

"Here?" Doubt filled her expression as she looked around at the shadowed terrace, but by the time she looked back at him, assurance and certainty had replaced the doubt. "Fine."

Without another word, he took her hand, drew her into his arms, and began to slowly move with her. The laughter and voices of the party gradually receded until there was only the music . . . and her—to see, to feel, to smell, to want.

He danced her in and out of the shadows, following the soft, melodic music that drifted on the currents of the scented air. And Kylie moved with him with such grace and ease, an onlooker would have made the mistaken assumption that she'd danced with him many times before.

In reality he'd only danced with her once before, on the night of her high school graduation. Now, on her twenty-first birthday, he was dancing with her again. It would be the last time, he reflected grimly, because he'd be damned if he would dance with her on her wedding day.

But tonight, and for this moment, he was holding her in his arms, and she was dancing with him, only him. Her hand moved restlessly over the shoulder of his evening jacket as she stared up at him, her beautiful lips slightly parted, her gaze fixed on his.

With his hand at her back, he applied the lightest of pressures to pull her toward him, and to his surprise, she seemed to flow into him, filling in empty spaces he hadn't even known he'd had. And just when he thought she couldn't get any closer to him, she did, pressing into him until her breasts were crushed against his chest and her body fit snugly against his pelvis. He'd thought she might draw away from him as soon as she felt his arousal through the fragile material of her gown, but not his Kylie.

She moved as one with him, her skirt floating outward like a cloud of silk. Her face raised to his, and the warm night air blew soft wisps of her pale hair onto her face.

In the shadows once again, he slowed their dance steps until they were doing little more than swaying together, back and forth, close, so close, and then even closer.

He was hopelessly mesmerized by her and everything she was.

Brave, she was so brave, never once allowing her gaze to drop from his, even after she felt his hard need. God, she was so sweet, softening the curves and mounds of her body until he'd swear she was melting into the hard angles of his body. *God help him*, she was irresistible—what in the hell was he going to do about her?

Somewhere along the line, he must have blinked. He hadn't known she was capable of crawling inside him and learning his innermost desires. He hadn't suspected that her innermost desires might possibly match his.

Slowly she drew her hand from his. Standing on her tiptoes, she slid her hand around his neck until her hands met at its back beneath his hair. Then she murmured his name and he felt the warmth of her breath on his lips.

He groaned inwardly. In the dangerous heat of combat, he had total command over his body. His emotions turned to ice and his pulse remained perfectly steady. But with Kylie in his arms, his heart was beating out of control and everything in him felt hot.

Rules that he'd tried to follow over the last few years suddenly vanished, his conscience abruptly silenced. Barely aware of what he was doing, he lowered his head and captured her soft lips with his.

He felt her quiver slightly, then she opened her mouth wider to accept his thrusting tongue. He'd often imagined what she would taste like, but his imagination and the reality weren't even close. She tasted of perfumed sensuality, burning femininity, and heady champagne. Just one taste of her and he was intoxicated, and he took more than one taste, much more.

Only silk separated his hands from her flesh, and if she were anyone else, he'd push her back against a pillar and take her right then and there and damned the party going on just yards away.

But she wasn't just anyone. She was Kylie Damaron and he'd known her too long and respected her too much to do something that carried such an inherent risk of embarassing her.

Yet his strength to resist her was nearly gone, his

determination to keep their relationship on a friendly basis was seriously weakened, and the pain urging him to have her was growing with each breath he took.

With an audible groan, he tore his lips from hers and pushed her away from him until she was at arm's length. She looked up at him, her expression soft and dazed with desire, and the thought flashed through his mind that her expression was probably the most dangerous thing he'd ever seen.

"Walk away, Kylie," he said, his voice deadly quiet. "Walk away while you've still got the chance."

She took a step back from him, but went no farther. Her breasts rapidly rose and fell beneath the blue silk as she tried to pull air into her lungs. Her skin was flushed, her lips were swollen, her eyes were huge. He'd never seen her look more beautiful or more desirable.

"Meet me at the studio at three," she said. "If the party isn't over by then, I'll end it." And then with a billow of blue silk and a wafting of perfume, she was gone, leaving him stunned.

Had he heard her right? Did he dare even believe he had?

He turned on his heel, went in the back door of the house and straight out the front door. Several young men who had been hired to handle the parking rushed toward him, eager to retrieve his car and collect a tip, but one by one they got a look at his hard expression and retreated.

He turned the key in the ignition, and the engine leaped to life. Once away from Abigail's estate and out on the dark country road, he floored the accelerator, unaware and uncaring of where he was going.

The night was pleasant and cool, but he opened the windows and turned the air conditioner on so that it would blow straight into his face. He breathed deeply, needing the wind and the chilled air to cool the fire in his belly, on his skin, and in his mind. But it wasn't working, and no matter how fast he drove, he couldn't escape her words. *Meet me at the studio at three.*

Years ago, Joanna had had the studio built on the grounds of Abigail's estate so that she could have a place to work on her clothing designs over long week-ends and holidays and still be close to Kylie. But when Jo got married and moved to a neighboring estate, Kylie had converted the studio into a retreat for herself. During her college years she'd used it as a place to study, or to simply get away from the activity at the big house.

And now she wanted him to meet her there at three.

He glanced down at the speedometer and realized he'd let his speed fall off during the last few minutes. He jammed his foot to the floor and had the satisfaction of feeling the machine spring forward. Luckily he didn't meet much oncoming traffic, and when he drew too close to a town, he simply turned down another country road.

He had to keep going forward. Away. Far away.

Kylie didn't know what she was asking of him.

For the past few years when he'd been with Kylie, he'd spent much of his time fighting against his own sexual desires so that he could continue to treat her as he had for most of her life—like a little sister, whom he could love, and protect without complications.

No. Meeting her in the studio wouldn't work, because making love to her now would bring about a hundred complications that he wasn't ready for.

Besides, even if she wasn't the little sister of his best friends, he still couldn't treat her as he had the women before her—the women who understood and accepted, without him saying a word, that the present was all he could offer.

Sometimes the present lasted only hours, sometimes days. But in the time he had with a woman, he made sure there were never any regrets, only fun and mutual satisfaction. Then inevitably a call would come in with orders that would send him off in some new direction, and he'd leave without so much as a backward glance.

Kylie deserved much better than that.

He glanced at his watch. It was two A.M. He lifted his foot off the accelerator and gradually the car slowed to a stop.

A vision of Kylie entered in his mind—Kylie as she'd been right after their kisses, dazed and soft. What would she look like after he'd made love to her?

"*Damn it!*" He hit the steering wheel with his fist. "Damn it," he muttered softly. He wrenched the steering wheel around and headed back to Abigail's.

With minutes to go until three, David wandered around the studio, taking in the changes that Kylie had made. Gone were Jo's drafting tables, along with her portfolios, mounds of fabric samples, and stacks of drawing tablets. Instead there were comfy-looking couches and chairs arranged around the fireplace. An afghan was thrown over the back of one couch. Books were stacked on a side table. A strand of pearls was strewn over another table. Several high-heeled shoes and a pair of sneakers were heaped in one corner, as if she'd kicked them off as soon as she entered.

Upstairs, the loft held a king-sized bed, heaped with pillows. And even after opening the French doors and windows, the entire studio still smelled of Kylie's perfume. He turned on a few of the ceiling fans to get the air moving.

The sounds of the party were quieting, but on the off chance that one of the party guests might wander in this direction, he didn't turn on any lights. Only Kylie's family and a few of her closest friends knew about the studio, and he didn't want to attract any undue attention by lighting up the place. Besides, moonlight poured from windows as tall as the two-story-high ceiling, making it very easy for him to see.

He rolled his shoulders, then bent his head from side to side to loosen his muscles. Kylie would be here soon. She would, that is, unless she'd had second thoughts.

But *if* she came, he planned to simply talk with her, to tell her that if she thought they were going to continue on with what had happened between them on the terrace, she was wrong.

And she had to hear it from him. It would hurt her too much, he reasoned, if she arrived and he wasn't there. At least this way he could gently explain his point of view, make her understand why it wouldn't work out, and then leave.

"David."

He turned around, then softly gasped. Kylie stood in the open doorway, drenched in moonlight, blue silk, and diamonds.

Unconsciously he held his hand up, palm out, as if to ward her off. "No."

A lovely, radiant smile spread across her face and she walked straight into his arms, just as she'd done when she was five years old. Except this time she was a grown woman and she looked up into his eyes without fear. "Yes," she murmured, then stood on tiptoe and kissed him. Lightly at first, then slowly, but surely, deepening the kiss.

He tried to resist, but it was like trying to stop a raging river with a dam of toothpicks. Impossible. Futile. Hopeless.

Before he knew what was happening, his arms had closed around her, lifting her off her feet, and he was returning her kisses with all the pent-up passion he'd held inside for so long. Too long. His mind shut down as heat rose, desire soared, passion escalated, and clothes disappeared. Then they were on the carpet in front of the unlit fireplace making love—mind-blowing, soul-destroying, all-consuming, all-encompassing love.

Over the years, he'd denied himself of Kylie to the point that, without realizing it, he was actually starving for her. In fact he was so hungry for her, he never once took into account how small and delicate her body was. His mind was filled with the madness of wanting her, and he used no finesse, just power as he pulled his hips back and drove into her.

She made a sound—pleasure, pain, he didn't know. *Pain?* She'd been a virgin. The thought entered the haze of his mind, then was instantly dismissed when he felt her hips begin to move in rhythm with his. She was so tight around him that every move he made took him that much closer to ecstasy, and soon every time he penetrated her, Kylie gasped with unmistakable pleasure.

They made love as well as they'd danced together— as one and with a rhythm and boundless need they both understood.

After it was over and he was lying beside her, waiting for his breathing and heartbeat to steady and his mind to clear, he remembered the surprise he'd received. She'd been a virgin. The fact gave him a feeling of satisfaction that he couldn't explain then or now.

They made love once more that night. He'd scooped her into his arms and carried her up the spiral staircase to the moonlit bed. There they'd made love slower, taking the time to explore, each tasting, stroking, and learning about the textures and curves of the other's body. Words seemed superfluous. Only sensations and feelings had been important.

Dawn had found them asleep in each other's arms, but his training rarely let him fall deeply asleep. His job demanded that he be alert at all times, and the fact that he wasn't officially on a mission didn't affect his automatic response. The sound of his pager beeping downstairs was enough to awaken him. Reluctantly he'd extricated himself from Kylie's arms and quietly made his way down the stairs to the pager. He found a Code One alert flashing on the readout. He had to leave at once.

He quickly dressed and then went upstairs once more. Kylie was fast asleep and he decided not to wake her. A coward's act, maybe. Probably. But he wasn't sure what he wanted to say to her.

The few hours they'd spent together had happened so fast, though in other ways it had been a long time coming. Volatile emotions and needs still careened through him, unchecked, undisciplined, and leaving him with more questions than answers. On top of it all, there was nothing he could tell her about why he needed to leave so fast. His work was top secret.

So he'd settled for a quickly scrawled note that promised to get back in touch with her as soon as he could. The last thing he'd done was reach into his jacket pocket and pull out her birthday present, a heart-shaped sapphire that dangled from a delicate golden chain.

When he'd found the stone in Burma, he'd immediately known that Kylie was the only woman in the world who should wear it. He'd had it cut and set specially for her, but now he wasn't even going to get to see her expression when she first saw it. Disappointed, but also resigned, he dropped the stone on the note, then bent to press a light kiss on her lips.

Unfortunately, the mission had taken longer than anyone had expected, and the next time he'd seen her had been eight months later at Abigail's annual Christmas Eve party. Kylie had barely looked at him, her laughter had been brittle, and she'd had a young man on each arm. When he'd approached her and asked if he could speak with her privately, she'd looked at him as if he were little more than vermin and told him they had nothing to talk about.

Her brush-off had been painful. It had also sliced into his pride and made him angry as hell. But more than that, it had confused him.

Perhaps it was all for the best, he'd reasoned, trying to convince himself. Eight months was a long time. Maybe she'd decided she didn't want a sexual relationship with him. Maybe she'd grown tired of waiting for him and found someone else, someone her own age who could commit completely to her.

But even as he'd thought this, bile had risen in his throat.

His initial response was to dive back into his work. For quite a few years, his organization had been sending him out on their most dangerous missions, which suited him just fine. As far as he was concerned, the more danger the better, because it made him focus on what he was doing rather than remembering Kylie.

But living with danger on a daily basis had a way of putting things into perspective. Eventually he forgot the injury to his pride, and after a while, his pain eased.

The next time he was home, he approached Kylie again. Unfortunately, the results were the same. She hadn't changed her mind, and she had no intention of talking to him one-on-one. Months later, he'd tried one last time to be alone with her so that they could hash things out. Without a word, she'd turned and left the room.

After that, he gave up trying. When he saw her, he was polite but cool, and he never again tried to speak to her privately. Those precious hours on the night of her party had been the last time he'd had more than five minutes in her company until last night.

Still, he'd never been able to get her or those few hours they'd spent together, locked in each other's arms, out of his mind, though God knows he'd tried.

And then three months ago something unexpected had happened.

He'd been laid up in Paris and had called Sin, expecting a shooting-the-breeze type of conversation like they usually had. But when Sin had told him that Kylie was on her way to meet with Molinari, something had snapped inside him.

Protective instincts he'd thought long dead had come alive, stronger than ever. Old feelings had flared to life, hot and powerful. He'd immediately placed a call to her to try to talk her out of the plan. It hadn't worked.

But even after he'd learned that the meeting had gone well and that Kylie would soon be on her way home, he still couldn't stop worrying about her.

Suddenly he found himself envisioning what his world would be like if something happened to Kylie, and the picture he saw in his head and felt in his gut had made him ill. That was when it hit him. He still deeply cared for her.

As a result, he'd decided that during this trip home, Kylie would damn well hear him out and talk to him, even if he had to kidnap her.

But none of his decisions had included her being shot at.

Slowly exhaling, he refocused on the sky that was steadily lightening. The new day was beginning.

He turned away from the window and reached for the phone on Kylie's desk.

FIVE

A cup of coffee in her hand, Kylie opened the door of her office. One step later she stopped. David was leaning back in her leather chair, his shoes propped on an open desk drawer, his legs crossed at the ankles. He was talking on the phone he held between his shoulder and cheek and was taking notes in a small notebook that lay open on one thigh.

Funny, she thought. She'd hardly seen him at all in the last seven years and now she couldn't seem to walk into a room without him being there.

David glanced over at her and raised a hand of acknowledgment. "Thanks, Louis, I'd appreciate that." He paused as he listened. "Right. I definitely think that's the best way to go. Thanks again. 'Bye."

He hung up the phone and leaned back in the chair, not bothering to remove his feet from her drawer. "Looks like you beat Clifford in. He'll be mortified."

She shrugged. "It's still early."

"I know," he said, studying her. She looked more fragile than usual this morning, her skin paler, more translucent. As for the smudges of darkness directly beneath her eyes, they could have been explained by a slip of an eyeliner pencil, but he knew better. "Weren't you able to sleep?"

"I slept a little." She sank into one of the chairs in front of her desk and sipped at her coffee. "Who were you talking to?"

"A friend who may be able to help us figure out who was doing the shooting last night."

"And *why*, I hope."

"And why," he agreed. This morning her guard was back up, and the fact that he'd expected it didn't make it any easier for him to handle. Last night their shared experience and memories had brought them closer, but this morning reality had separated them again.

She gestured with her coffee cup. "I brought this from my apartment, but if I'd known you would be here, I would have brought another cup."

"No problem. I'll grab some later."

"Okay. So why are you doing your calling from my office, with your feet on my desk?"

"I'm here because I wanted to see you first thing."

"Why?"

He swung his long legs off the drawer, closed it, and straightened. "Strange as it may seem to you, Kylie, I wanted to see what kind of night you had and how you're feeling this morning. And before you ask why again, I'll tell you that it's because you were shot at last night."

"I wasn't going to ask why. Being shot at is something I'm not liable to forget."

"Then tell me how you're feeling."

"Fine. Just fine."

She wasn't feeling fine at all, he reflected grimly. She was all nerves.

She finished her coffee and leaned forward to set the cup down. "How about yourself? It looks as if you've been here awhile. Did you get any sleep?"

"Enough."

"Good." She spread out her hands. "Then I guess that about covers the subject of how we both are."

"Right," he said, studying her carefully. "Except you forgot to say that you're holding your feelings in so tightly that if you breathe wrong, you may shatter."

She shook her head. "I may look like I might shatter, but you should know by now that I won't."

"Yeah," he murmured. "You'd think I *would* know that by now, wouldn't you?" Slipping the notebook inside his jacket pocket, he stood. "What's your schedule today?"

"Unless something unforeseen happens, I'll be here all day."

"Then I'll probably see you later."

Slowly he rounded the desk, but he couldn't make himself leave just yet. He felt a strong compulsion to stay and soothe away her fears, just as he'd done for most of her life. And he wanted to talk with her as they had last night, gently and softly, and then make love the same way. Irrational, he thought. Completely irrational. But he'd noticed long ago that he was irrational only when it came to her.

"David?"

"Yes?"

She rose. "Where are you going right now?"

"I'm going to have breakfast with a friend of mine, Scott Hewitt. You may end up meeting him. If it turns out he can't make it home for Christmas, I'm going to invite him to Abigail's party."

"You're going *out* for breakfast?"

"Yes."

"Are you sure that's wise?"

"Wise?" He frowned. "Kylie, nothing is going to happen to me, if that's what you're afraid of."

A forced smile appeared. "No. Of course not."

"Then what's wrong?" he asked, watching her carefully. "I need to get out and run down some things."

She shrugged. "Forget that I said anything. It's just that—"

"Ms. Damaron!" Clifford hurried into the office, then abruptly braked at the sight of David. Taking in a deep breath, he concentrated on Kylie. "I'm sorry, Ms. Damaron. I didn't know you were going to be in this early—I would have planned to arrive much earlier."

"It's all right," she said calmly. "Don't worry about it."

"But—"

She picked up her coffee cup and thrust it into Clifford's hand. "Would you mind making up a pot of coffee?"

"No, not at all." Obviously relieved to have a task, Clifford rushed toward the door.

Kylie gazed after him. "Clifford?"

He halted. "Yes, Ms. Damaron?"

"Relax. You're doing a fine job."

Clifford looked startled, then slowly smiled. "Thank you, Ms. Damaron. I'll get the coffee."

When they were alone again, David looked down at her. "What were you about to say, Kylie?"

"What? Oh . . ." She shook her head. "I was just going to say that if you find out anything, anything at all, please let me know."

"Sure." For a few moments, right before Clifford had rushed in, he could have sworn she was about to say she was worried about him, or something similar. She hadn't, though, and it was all right. He didn't need words when he had the memory of last night's kiss. Lord, how he'd wanted her, and she'd just started responding to him when he'd broken it off. He'd had to.

He hadn't wanted the first time they made love in seven years to be on a night when she was feeling afraid, vulnerable, and exposed. If they ever made love again, and he prayed they would, he wanted her to make the choice with a clear head so that she'd have no regrets the next morning. He couldn't go through that again. He wouldn't.

On an impulse, he stepped forward and pressed a light, lingering kiss to her lips. "See you later."

The first call Kylie received that morning came from Joanna.

"I would have called you last night, honey, but I spoke to Jonah and he said that you were okay, but needed to get some sleep, and that when they left, David had stayed with you."

"That's right," she said, her tone wry. Her family had always considered her protected when she was with David, and as far as her physical safety went, it was true. An hour or so after David had left last night, she'd peeked out her door to see if he really had left his front door open. He had. She could trust him with her life, but not her heart.

His kisses, both last night's and this morning's, had left her feeling as if she were in genuine peril. If he hadn't broken off the kiss last night, she wasn't certain she would have had the strength to do it herself.

But *he'd* had the strength. Why had he kissed her as if he weren't going to be able to get enough of her, then stopped right at the point when she'd been ready to take the next step? And afterward, she hadn't been able to find any sign of the kiss's heated emotions. Not on his face and not in his eyes. Had it been a game to him? Or perhaps revenge for the cool way she'd acted toward him for the last seven years?

She touched her lips where his had been only an hour before, then caught herself and went on to answer Jo's questions regarding what had happened.

"Honey, do you want Cale, the kids, and me to come into the city and be with you?"

Jo was thinking of her, but she was thinking of Jo. "As much as I'd love to have you all with me, I really think you'd be better off there. I'm sure that Cale is doing his usual brilliant job of keeping you and your babies safe."

Jo laughed. "At times like this, when there's a chance our family might be in danger, he becomes positively manic in his efforts."

Kylie chuckled. "I knew I liked that man."

"Yes, but we'd be just as safe there at the Tower with you."

True, Kylie, thought. As long as Jo stayed inside the Tower. But something might go wrong on the trip in. And if Jo was here, she'd definitely want to go out. No. The person who was trying to kill her was still out there, waiting for his chance, and if Jo was anywhere around her, she might not be safe.

"You and those beautiful babies of yours stay close to home and we'll see each other Christmas Eve."

"Okay, honey, if you're sure."

"I am."

If anything happened to Jo and Cale, their little ones would be alone. She'd once been small like they were, completely vulnerable to acts beyond her understanding and control, and she couldn't stand the idea that the same thing might happen to Jo's children.

"And listen, don't worry about me. I probably have more guards on me than the President. I'll see you on Christmas Eve. 'Bye."

As the day went on, she was able to get some of her business matters settled in between the parade of cousins checking in with her almost constantly. It made her feel more secure that they were staying in, as she was.

Allesandro called about two. "How are you?"

She inwardly sighed. She was getting sick of that question, but it certainly wasn't Allesandro's fault. "I'm fine. Have you been able to find out anything?"

"Nothing so far."

She forced a laugh. "Well, I suppose that's good. It means things are just as you thought and that you've got a tight lid on the people around you and your business."

"But that doesn't keep me from worrying about you. Has your family been able to find out anything?"

"No, I'm afraid not, but I'll let you know when they do."

"Kylie, the police showed up at the restaurant last night. The gunfire was reported, as I knew it would be, so I waited for them and answered their questions."

"Why on earth did you wait for them?" she asked with genuine concern. "Your people could have gotten you out of there before they showed up."

"Maybe, but I wanted to keep your name out of it. So as far as the police know, those bullets were meant for me."

She let out a long, weary breath. "That wasn't necessary."

"I thought it was."

"I'm so sorry, Allesandro. That's not going to help your pursuit for legitimacy one bit. The police will have more reason than ever to suspect you."

"So what's new? They'll always suspect me no matter what I do. At any rate, it's nothing I can't handle, and needless to say, the police won't spend a lot of time and trouble looking for a person who would want to shoot me." Dry humor lay beneath his words. "In fact, if they did find him, they'd probably give him the key to the city."

She sighed. "Allesandro . . ."

"What's the matter, Kylie?"

"I hate it that you had to put yourself in jeopardy for me."

He chuckled. "Staying and talking to the police is *not* putting myself in jeopardy."

She closed her eyes and shook her head. "Allesandro, listen to me. Worry about yourself. Take more care than usual with your own safety, and concentrate on keeping yourself on the path that you've started for your business. Whatever you do, don't worry about me. I'm going to be fine."

He was silent for several moments. "All right, Kylie. I'll do my best to do as you wish, but that doesn't change the fact that I still want to know when your family comes up with anything, anything at all."

"I'll let you know. 'Bye, Allesandro." She hung up the phone and pushed back from her desk.

David had been the only one who hadn't checked in with her, at least not since this morning, and for some reason she'd expected to hear from him.

Or maybe the truth was that she *wanted* to hear from him. He was on the outside, unprotected as far as she knew. She should feel reassured that his profession was danger, because it meant he knew how to handle trouble. But she wasn't reassured about him and his profession. She never had been.

Lion strolled into her office at around four to drop off the list of stores that had agreed to stay open after hours for them. "We'll all be driven to and from the stores, and I'm sure we'll probably want to go separately, since we all won't be interested in the same shops. Needless to say, security will be the highest."

Leaning back in her chair, she nodded. Lion had golden eyes that changed from dark to light, depending on his moods. His sister, Yasmine, had beautiful amber eyes. But David's eyes were almost solid gold and their color never changed, only their intensity.

"What's the matter, baby?"

She rubbed her forehead. "I'm just a little tired, that's all. Between telling people I'm all right, I actually got quite a bit of work accomplished. I think I'll close up shop for the day and go upstairs to lie down, maybe take a nap."

"Good idea. Do you want me to come sit with you?"

His offer drew a smile from her, along with the thought that she must look worse than she felt. "Thank you, but no, thanks. As tired as I am, I'm sure I'll drop right off to sleep."

He nodded. "Okay, then, but if you want someone to talk to, remember I'm only a phone call away."

"I'll remember."

"Then I'll see you at nine if not before. We're all going to meet in the main foyer."

Their main foyer was a spacious area between the two elevator banks on the floor that held her apartment, along with Wyatt's and two others. At times, they all gathered there for drinks after business hours. "Lion, have you heard from David?"

"Yeah. He checked in a couple of hours ago to say that he had a lead he's trying to run down. Since he hasn't called back, I can only assume he either ran into a dead end or he's still checking it out."

Or something could have happened to him. "Does he have security with him?"

Lion shook his head. "That's not his way. Security

would only slow him down. At any rate, he'll be here at nine to go shopping with us."

She nodded. She didn't know why she'd expected David to check in with her. But she had.

A large, round mahogany table stood in the center of the foyer, holding an immense crystal bowl filled with red poinsettias and metallic beads. Twinkling lights and silver and gold ornaments adorned the Christmas tree that was set in front of the window. More poinsettias were banked beneath the tree.

She'd have to remember to drop a note of praise to the decorator who'd done it, Kylie decided as she tossed her coat onto the back of a chair and scanned the foyer. Her cousins were all assembled. Only David wasn't there.

At least she felt rested and more relaxed. She'd managed to get a couple of hours' sleep and had prepared herself a light supper. Afterward, she'd had a bath, then slipped into beige slacks with a matching sweater and low-heeled walking shoes.

Sin came over and pressed a loving kiss to her cheek. "You're looking much better than you did earlier."

She grinned. "Between you and Lion, I get the distinct impression I looked like a hag today."

Joining them, Jonah laughed. "Oh, yeah, I noticed that right away and spread the news. You'll find the information in all of tomorrow's papers."

She chuckled. "Watch it, Jonah. I haven't bought your Christmas present yet."

"Really?" Taking her arm, he stepped closer and spoke in a playfully low and confidential voice. "In that case, I've had my eye on a snazzy crocodile golf bag. Gucci, as I recall."

Her brows arched. "Crocodile?"

He nodded, his demeanor serious, his golden brown eyes filled with laughter. "I've given a lot of thought to the matter and I think that crocodile will send exactly the right signal to other golfers."

As she knew he wanted, she bit. "And what signal would that be?"

"Why, that when I step onto a golf green, I'm to be *feared*, of course."

"Of course." She patted his chest. "Get back to me when you actually *learn* to play golf and we'll talk."

His hands suddenly flew to his chest and he staggered backward. "*Oooh*—that hurt, Kylie. I mean, that *really* hurt."

Lion appeared at her side. "Allow me to escort you away from this man and over to the bar." He threw a jokingly distrustful look over at Jonah. "I don't know how he got in here anyway. He obviously painted that silver streak in his hair."

"Obviously," she said, going along with her cousins. She knew they were worried about her and were trying to make her feel better. "And naturally you have no ulterior motive in saving me?"

Lion did his best to look shocked. "Absolutely not! However, if you just happen to see the new Armani—"

She help up her hand. "*Stop.* I've already bought your gift."

He visibly brightened. "Oh, yeah? What is it?" He

glanced at the security man who was doubling behind the bar. "A champagne cocktail for the incredibly lovely lady, please."

She shook her head. "All the compliments in the world aren't going to help you. You'll find out Christmas day, just like you always do."

In the years since their parents had been killed, their custom had been to throw a giant slumber party at Abigail's after her Christmas Eve party, then open their presents together on Christmas morning. But now that quite a few of them had married and had started having children, they all stayed at home on Christmas morning, then gathered at Abigail's in the afternoon for presents and dinner.

Lion handed her the champagne cocktail. "You were right, Jonah," he said in a loud voice. "She's a hard woman."

"Where's David? I thought you said he would be here."

"Oh, he called around seven. Said he wasn't sure if he could make it, but was definitely going to try. I read him the list of shops, but he was only interested in a few."

"Oh." She told herself she was glad she didn't have to see him tonight. This way she didn't have to guard her emotions in case he might accidently touch her, or perhaps even kiss her again.

Suddenly, from behind her, slender, golden-skinned arms were thrown around her and she heard a laughing voice. "Hey, sweetie, how are you doing?"

She knew before she turned around that her cousin Yasmine had just arrived. "I'm good," she said with a big smile and a hug. "And now that you're here, I'm even better. What a *wonderful* surprise." She glanced behind Yasmine to see the tall, computer-genius Texan that her cousin had married, Rio Thornton.

He grinned. "Do I get a hug?"

"You bet," she said, going into his arms with delight. "I wasn't certain I'd get to see you two before Christmas Eve."

"When we learned guards were flying in, we decided to just hop on the plane and fly home a couple of days early."

Kylie nodded, understanding completely. Yasmine had done it for her so that she wouldn't worry about the two of them.

"Besides," Rio drawled, "Yaz couldn't stand being left out of this shopping trip."

"He's right," Yasmine said with a laugh, though her lighthearted tone was not echoed in her eyes.

Yasmine was concerned about her, and Kylie hated that she was.

A radio crackled. Tim was standing by one of the elevators, speaking into his radio. When he finished, he looked around. "Okay, everyone," he said in a raised voice. "They're ready for us downstairs." He pointed to the four elevators, two on either side of the foyer. "We'll all go down at the same time with security in each elevator."

Jonah spoke up. "Sin and I are heading for F.A.O. Schwarz first. Anyone want to go with us?"

Kylie put down her drink and reached for her coat. "Not me." Like the others, she'd already done her shopping for her family's growing brood of little ones.

"But that reminds me. Both of your wives called me today and asked me to remind you two *not* to come home with the electric train sets you've been talking about. Your babies are too little yet."

Sin laughed. "Yeah, we know."

Jonah grinned. "But *we're* not."

Kylie shook her head. "Please tell Jolie and Jillian that I tried." She stepped into the elevator with Yasmine and Rio, along with two security men.

"Where are you going first, Kylie?" Yasmine asked with a look at Rio. "Maybe we'll tag along."

She caught the look that passed between the Yasmine and her husband. "Listen, you two. Quit worrying about me. I really am okay. And if you two have any requests, you'd better give them to me now, because you're high on my list."

Yasmine tossed her braid over her shoulder. "Well, now that you asked, check to see if Armani has started making maternity outfits."

Kylie's eyes widened and she let out a yelp of happy surprise. "That's *fabulous*, Yaz!"

"And I'll take something tasteful in tranquilizers," Rio said dryly. "As large a quantity as possible, please."

"The news has been a little hard on his nerves," Yasmine said with a loving smile up at her husband. "If he had his way, he would be carrying me around on a satin pillow."

Kylie shrugged. "Hey, go with it while you can. By the way, am I the last to know?"

"Actually, you're the first," Yasmine said, "and you're *not* to tell a soul. We're going to make the announcement Christmas afternoon when we're all together and it's just the family."

The elevator came to a stop and the doors slid open onto the underground parking area. With military precision, the guards quickly escorted them to their appointed cars.

Tim appeared at her side. "Kylie, I'm with you for the evening. There will also be an extra car with us."

Since she had been the target of last night's attack, it made sense that she would get the heaviest security. Still, Tim's pronouncement dampened her excitement over Yasmine's news.

Tim guided her to one of the cars and saw that she was settled in the back seat before he took his place beside the driver.

He threw a glance at her over his shoulder. "Where to?" She reached into her purse for her list. "Let's first hit Fifth Avenue and the designer emporiums. Just start driving while I scan my list and I'll let you know which place to stop first."

"Okay." Tim nodded at the driver and the car started moving out into the bright lights and constant movement of the city. Tim looked back at her. "Just for my own information, do you have some idea of where you want to end up?"

Without looking up from her list, she nodded. "More than likely at Saks."

"Okay, then, just sit back and don't worry about a thing."

To stop worrying was easier said than done. Even with all of their resources, her family hadn't yet been able to find out who had tried to kill her the night before. Not only that, Allesandro, with the different type of resources at his disposal, hadn't been able to come up with anything either. That left David, and all she'd heard from him that day had come secondhand— he was following a trail.

What trail? Where did it lead? Was he still following that trail or had he hit a dead end? And *why* hadn't he called her?

SIX

Someone was watching her.

The heels of her walking shoes sounded startlingly loud, Kylie reflected, trying to shake the feeling as she made her way across the polished floor of the store to a display of men's leather gloves.

Bright ceiling lights reflected on gleaming glass countertops and stainless steel racks. White doves and pearls were the Christmas decoration of choice for this store. Tiny fairy lights twinkled among the elegant trees. Mannequins draped in every imaginable holiday ensemble posed around the trees. The audio system played Christmas carols that floated eerily into all the empty corners and spaces in the store.

Someone was watching her.

The hairs on the back of her neck were standing on end, and it wasn't because of the music or the almost empty store. Someone was watching her and it was someone other than the people she knew were guarding her. The feeling had started at the last shop and she couldn't shake it.

"Ms. Damaron?"

She started, even though the manager had spoken in a low voice. He was a slight man, currently wearing the same anxious expression as the sales associate beside him, an older woman with a well-cared-for face, who had been helping Kylie. "Yes?"

"Is there something wrong with the gloves? Perhaps the size? The color? You've only to tell us and I am sure we'll be able to find exactly what you want."

With vague surprise, she glanced down at the pair of men's leather gloves in her hands. She'd forgotten that she'd picked them up. She'd been thinking of David when she'd first seen them, wondering where he was and if he might need a new pair of gloves.

She dropped them. A pair of men's leather gloves was definitely not on her list. "The gloves are fine. Just give me a moment while I think about what I have left to buy."

"Certainly." The manager motioned to the sales associate, who moved to his side, and they both backed off several feet.

She shifted her position slightly so that she could see Tim. He was standing just outside the front door, his back to her, speaking on his cell phone. The car, parked at the curb, had another guard standing beside it. Tim also had all other exits covered. No one could get in or out without going through a guard. So why did she feel so uneasy?

The shopping had gone easily enough and she only had a couple of gifts yet to get. During the last two hours, she'd run into her cousins at different stores, but so far she was the only one here. Was that why she was feeling jumpy? No, that didn't make sense. An empty store wasn't enough to spook her and she'd felt the same way at the last store, where she'd run into Rio and Yasmine. She simply needed to get a grip on her feelings and get her shopping over with.

She turned toward the manager and the sales associate. "I'd like to see what you have in cashmere shawls."

The anxiousness drained out of both of their faces and was replaced by an eagerness to please. "Right this way," the manager said.

With a last reassuring look toward Tim, Kylie followed them. The shawls were located in the center of the store, along with scarves, purses, jewelry, and perfume.

She instantly saw what she wanted, an oversized cashmere shawl that Yasmine could grab up and throw around her nightgown in the middle of the night when her baby cried. "Do you have this in a golden brown?" she asked, thinking of Yasmine's eyes.

The manager frowned, but the sales associate nodded. "I'm almost certain we received another order of these shawls a day or two ago, and there very well may be a golden brown in the back. I know it does come in that color."

"I'll come with you," the manager told the older woman. "With the two of us looking, we should find it in no time at all." He glanced at Kylie. "With your permission?"

"Of course," she said and wandered down an aisle

in the fine jewelry department. Within a minute she found exactly what she wanted for Abigail. A big, slightly gaudy gold cuff bracelet with big red stones set around it.

The feeling came again. *Someone was definitely watching her*.

She whirled around and quickly scanned what she could see of the store. But there was no one there. No one at all.

She rubbed her forearms, chiding herself. There was no reason for her to be so apprehensive. She was well guarded, but for some reason she couldn't shake the feeling that she wasn't alone. Someone was definitely watching her.

She studied the store once again. Displays and distance hid what might be beneath the counters. Christmas trees blocked other views.

Footsteps.

Coming toward her.

Icy fear gripped her. Her heart thudded heavily. Get hold of yourself, Kylie. The footsteps had to belong to the manager, or the sales associate, or even both.

"Kylie?"

She swung around, then, seeing who it was, collapsed back against the glass counter with relief. "*David!* My God, David, you nearly scared me to death."

His brow knitted. "Why?"

She wrapped her arms around herself. "I know this is going to sound irrational, but I've been feeling like someone is watching me, and then I heard your footsteps coming toward me and I—"

"Wait," he said, his big body tensing. "Slow down. What do you mean, you've been feeling like someone is watching you?"

She shrugged. "Just that. It started in the store before this one and . . . Oh, never mind. I know it doesn't make sense. It's late and I've just spent two jam-packed hours of power shopping. I'm probably just tired. Is this your last store?"

"Yes," he said, scanning the store with an intensity that put her own survey to shame.

"Mine too."

"I know. I talked to Tim a while ago and found out where you were." The gold of his eyes was at full wattage as he continued to survey the store. "Did you tell Tim what you were feeling?"

"No. Look, David, don't pay any attention to what I just said. Obviously I've been letting my imagination run away from me."

"Since when have you ever let your imagination run away from you?"

She glanced up at him and saw that a gun had appeared in his right hand and his cell phone in his left. "Kylie, get down behind that counter and stay there until I say it's all right for you to come out."

His voice was low and perfectly calm, his hands steady, but she could feel herself begin to tremble. Then her training kicked in and she did as he said without a word. She hurried to the spot he had indicated and knelt on the floor. A second later she heard him speaking into the phone. "Tim, get in here. I think we've got trouble."

Suddenly glass cases all around her started to explode in a hail of automatic gunfire. Glass, mirror, and merchandise rained down over her. She pressed her face into her thighs, making her body into as tight a ball as possible, and held her hands on each side of her face to protect her eyes from the flying glass.

She could have done a better job of protecting her eyes and head if she could have thrown her coat over herself, but she was still wearing it. It all seemed so surreal. She was in one of the most upscale department stores in the world, thinking of ways to protect her eyes, because World War III had just broken out amid the very finest of jewelry, perfumes, satins, and silks.

But she knew better than to jump up from her hiding place and try to help. She had no weapon and she'd only end up being a burden and a distraction for both David and Tim, who were doing their best to protect her.

From her position, she had only her hearing to rely on. Strangely enough, after the initial outburst of fire, the bullets seemed to be hitting away from her, as if the focus of the deadly guns were now aimed somewhere else. It meant that David had moved away from her so as to draw the fire to himself.

David was protecting her, but who would protect him?

The battle continued and seemed to go on for an hour, though in real time she knew it had started mere minutes before.

Someone screamed. The sales associate, Kylie

thought. Kylie hoped she and the manager would have enough sense to hide in the back until the shooting stopped.

"*One down*," David shouted at Tim, and the gunfire continued. So there had been more than one person lying in wait for her. But *who? Why?*

Then, as suddenly as the gunfire had started, it stopped, leaving a startling silence.

She heard two people moving around. Please let it be David and Tim, she prayed. *Please* let it be them.

"Do you recognize them?" It was Tim. He was all right, which meant that David *had* to be.

"No," she heard David say, "but then I didn't expect to."

Slowly, she pushed herself up to a kneeling position. Glass sluiced off her. With her hands over her face, she shook her head and more glass flew off her. She did it one more time, then a big hand reached down for her. She took it.

"Are you okay?" David asked.

"Yes," she said, gingerly picking glass off her coat sleeve, "but then I wasn't the one out in the open." She glanced at him, and what she saw stunned her. If she had never seen David until this moment, she would run screaming with fear. He looked terrifyingly ruthless and menacing, and she realized she was seeing the toll of the firefight written on his face. "How are *you?*"

Without answering, he took her face in his hands and stared intently at her as he rubbed his thumbs back and forth over her smooth skin. "Thank God," he whispered. "Thank God you're all right." He closed his eyes for a moment, inhaled a deep, shaky breath, then looked at her again.

"David . . . ?"

"Your face isn't cut, but . . ." He captured her hands and lifted them so he could examine the cuts that patterned her hands with traces of blood. "You need to get these seen to."

"They're not bad. I'll treat them when I get home."

"There was so much glass," he said, frowning as he picked a piece of glass out of her hair, then another. "When you get home, you may discover more cuts. Make sure you rinse them thoroughly and use an antibiotic cream. And if they're very deep, they may need stitches."

"I'll take care of it, I promise. Now tell me how you are."

"Me?" he asked, surprised. "I'm standing in front of you, aren't I?"

The aggravating thing was, he really thought that was all he needed to say. "That's not what I meant."

Tim appeared. "We need to get you out of here before the authorities show up, Kylie."

"But—"

"Go, Kylie," David said, all business once more. "I'm going to slip out of here myself. Tim, who do you plan to leave behind to deal with the authorities?"

"I'm going to do that myself. I want to make sure there won't be any problems."

"Thanks."

With a hand on her elbow, Tim was maneuvering her toward the front door when Kylie saw the manager picking his way among the debris, his face paste-white.

Beside him, the sales associate, clearly in shock, moved like a zombie, but she was clutching the golden brown shawl to her breast, the search for which had probably saved her life.

"You found the shawl," Kylie said and was surprised to hear that her voice sounded normal. "I'll take it. Please charge it to my account along with the other things I selected, gift-wrap them, and send them to my apartment in the morning. Oh, and the same with the gold cuff bracelet with the red stones in the case right over there." She gestured.

"They're rubies ma'am," the manager said slowly, his voice without expression.

"Yes, I know," she said, her tone kind. "Thank you so much for your help this evening, and I'm sorry for all the mess. Naturally, you won't receive any blame and everything will be taken care of."

The manager swallowed. "We're always happy to be of service, Ms. Damaron."

Tim and David walked her out the front door to the car.

David bent down and opened the rear door. "Kylie, you said you thought someone was watching you in the last store too?"

"That's right."

He exchanged glances with Tim. "Then they also had a team there. They're probably gone by now, but Tim . . . ?"

"I'll have someone check it out."

"Thanks, and tomorrow we'll take over."

She only understood a part of what they were saying, but she'd find out later. Right now she had something else on her mind. "Tim," she murmured as she settled into the car, "make sure someone takes care of the manager and the sales associate. They're not doing very well."

"I've already got them covered." Tim closed the door and went around to the front of the car to speak to her driver.

David leaned down and tapped on the window. She pushed the button and the window glided down. "Are you coming back to the Tower?"

He shook his head. "Not right now. I've got a few things I have to see to first, but I want to tell you two things. One—you've got excellent instincts. Never ignore them. And two—you can quit worrying. They're after me, not you."

David wasn't home yet. She'd tried Wyatt's number twice, but his machine had answered. Finally she'd opened her door so that she would be able to hear David when he came in. Kylie sipped at the brandy she'd poured herself and wandered over to the windows. Snow had started falling in big, wet flakes.

Where was he?

She'd already called Allesandro to tell him that she hadn't been the target after all. He'd been incredibly relieved. She wished she could be too.

She set her glass on a table and paced back to the front door. There was nothing or no one in the hall that she could see, though she knew guards were in the foyer at the elevators. Basically, a high-security alert continued to be in effect at the Tower, because David was still in residence.

She rubbed her arms and returned to the living room. She'd already changed into her gown and robe, but she hadn't even tried to go to sleep. She was too keyed up, too tense and afraid. Instead, she'd started a fire and slid some smoky jazz into her CD player.

She should be feeling an enormous relief now that she knew for sure she hadn't been the target, and to some extent she was. A certain heaviness had been lifted from her, the heaviness of the fear and vulnerability she'd felt when she'd been told that an unknown someone in the darkness of the city wanted to kill her.

But now that heaviness had been replaced by a new fear and a new vulnerability that was coming at her from a different direction and had started the moment David had told her that *he* was the target, not her.

She shook her head at herself for feeling so anxious about him. Then, in the next moment, she told herself it was normal to care about whether someone in her life was going to be killed or not. Certainly worrying about him was much easier than loving him had been.

Loving David was something that had blazed to life in her heart starting that night so long ago when she was only five years old. That love had been easy.

But as the years had passed, that love had grown, branching off in a different direction, becoming more complex, until the night of her birthday party when the flames had roared out of control. That love had turned out to be impossible.

Still, she remembered every single thing about that night. She hadn't planned to ask David to meet her in the studio, but when they began dancing together and heat had begun to crawl through her veins, she'd known it was the right thing to do. Why not consummate the feelings that had been simmering between them for the last few years? Why not give her virginity to the man she'd loved all her life?

The next morning when she'd awakened alone, the answer to those two questions had hit her with a force she sometimes felt she still hadn't recovered from. She shouldn't have asked him to meet her in the studio. She shouldn't have made love with him. She shouldn't have even asked him to dance. She should have known he was too dangerous for her.

She remembered the joy she'd felt when she'd seen the sapphire heart, and she remembered the pain that had swooped down to envelop her as she'd read the note. Suddenly, emotional buttons she hadn't known existed were pushed until her insides ached and her heart broke.

Over the next few weeks, that initial pain disappeared beneath the waves of her almost constant state of fury at David for deserting her so abruptly.

Maybe it hadn't been as perfect for him as it had been for her, she'd tried to remind herself. She'd known that he was an experienced man. She'd accepted that, but he had been her first. If he hadn't known before, he'd learned it by the time he left. The least he could have done was wake her and tell her to her face that he had to leave. But he'd left her only a quickly scrawled note. For that she didn't think she could ever forgive him.

With every week that passed without hearing from

David, her fury at him for deserting her so abruptly grew until she literally collapsed beneath its weight. She kept the reason for her collapse private from everyone, saying only that she had the flu, and no one had any reason to doubt her. She slept for long hours at a time, hardly eating anything, and when she wasn't sleeping, she would lay quietly, thinking of nothing.

Finally, though, life began to return. Slowly she began to eat again and her mind began to work, sluggishly at first, then little by little both her body and her mind grew stronger until the day came when she realized why she'd had such a violent reaction.

It hadn't been David's fault. She supposed it hadn't been anyone's.

His note had psychologically jolted her back to that morning so long ago when she'd awakened to find her mother gone and only a note to tell her that she'd be back.

At the time she hadn't understood why her mother had left her so unexpectedly and without any warning. She also couldn't understand why her mother hadn't returned in four days as she had said in her note. She hadn't even been able to have the closure of seeing her mother and father one last time. The explosion that blew their plane apart had been so violent, their bodies had never been found.

She'd been left feeling frightened and abandoned, and even with all the love and care that was showered on her during that time, the feeling remained, like a hole in her that couldn't be filled. So in the middle of one stormy, black night, she'd run into the arms of an exotic-looking boy with startling golden eyes. Yet in the end, she'd been abandoned by him too. Or at least that was how she'd felt at the time.

She'd thrown herself into her work and the new responsibilities that had been bestowed on her after her graduation from college. But no matter how hard she worked, she couldn't forget him—not those fiery few hours they'd spent together, nor how much she still loved him.

But more importantly, she couldn't forget what David did for a living.

She and her cousins might routinely travel the globe, but they took extraordinary safety measures and never actively courted danger. David did.

His profession virtually ensured that, sooner or later, whichever woman he was with would wake up to a hastily scribbled note or even nothing at all. His profession also carried an astronomically high risk that the woman who loved him would one day receive a phone call and be told that David had been violently killed. And depending on the circumstances, there might be little or no chance that his body could be recovered.

She was smart enough to know that she couldn't go through something like that again. The first time it had happened to her, she'd had him to run to. But if it happened to him . . .

Months later, when she saw David again, she'd made sure that she protected herself from him by bringing two dates and playing up the fact for all it was worth. The next couple of times he came home and tried to speak with her, she'd turned an icy shoulder on him and walked away. Looking back, she realized she'd reacted childishly.

Considering her background and her relatively young age, she supposed some might say her reaction to David's note and her actions afterward had been perfectly normal. But she'd never been able to forgive herself quite so easily. When she'd finally realized the reason behind her reaction to his note, she'd been terribly embarrassed.

She should have been more mature about the matter, she'd told herself time and again. She should have had more courage. Yet as the years passed and David hadn't tried to contact her again, his absence became easier on her.

When she saw him, she was casually polite, nothing more, nothing less. If they talked, it was always in a group. If they smiled at each other, it was impersonal. And if her gaze happened to linger on him a second too long, it was only because she was mildly curious about his latest mission, his latest woman.

That was why his phone call from Paris three months earlier, telling her not to meet with Allesandro, had been such a shock. It had been a long time since he'd reached out to her on a one-to-one basis and she'd been curious. But when she'd heard his reason for calling, she'd become furious that he thought so little of her that he didn't think she could pull off the meeting.

And if pain had tried to seep into the mixture of her feelings, she'd quickly stopped it, and instead had put all her energies into making her meeting with Allesandro the success that she'd known it would be.

But now, three months later, she was waiting up for David so that she could make sure he was all right.

Where was he?

SEVEN

"Why is your door open?"

At the sound of David's sharp voice, Kylie whirled around from the fireplace. "I was waiting up for you."

"Why?" He crossed the room in a rush and put his hands on her shoulders. "Are you all right?"

She felt a tingle where his fingers gripped her. "I'm fine. The question is, how are you?"

He glanced around the room, then fixed her with a fierce gaze. "You should *never* leave your door open or unlocked. What were you thinking?"

"The guards are in the foyer, aren't they?"

"I don't care if you've got a whole division of guards in the foyer, you should keep your door closed and locked at all times."

"Look, David, I've never left the door open before, but tonight I wanted to make sure I heard you when you came in."

He abruptly released her shoulders. "That's not a good enough reason, Kylie. Don't do it again."

He was tense. *Very* tense. Thankfully, though, the ruthless, menacing expression she'd seen on his face after the firefight had vanished, yet he still appeared to be geared up for battle. His every word, his every move, overflowed with barely controlled nerves. "What's wrong, David? I mean, what's wrong other than the usual firefights and mayhem?"

"There's nothing else."

She folded her arms and regarded him with real concern. Whatever had put him in this shape was big. "I don't believe you. There's definitely something else wrong. Now tell me what it is."

"There's nothing else," he said again, this time with irritation.

She sighed and shook her head. He was giving her pat answers. "Okay, then tell me what's right."

The question got his attention as she'd hoped and his gaze cut to her. "You, Kylie. You're right."

His answer had come lightning-fast and in the same sharp tone he'd been using since he'd arrived, leaving her confused. Was he saying she'd been correct about something or had he meant something else? Not that it really mattered at this moment. "Okay, that covers me, now how about you? Are you all right?"

"I'm fine." Another pat answer, but then suddenly he exhaled a long breath and ran his hand around the back of his neck. "I'm tired."

"The surprise would be if you *weren't*. It's been a long and eventful day."

He glanced toward the entrance to her living room

as if he were considering leaving, then looked back at her. "You said you were waiting for me? Was there something you wanted?"

"Yes. I want answers and you look as if you could use a drink. How about a brandy? Sit down and I'll pour you one."

Without waiting for his answer, she crossed to the bar. Behind her, she sensed his hesitation, but then she heard him move.

"First let me lock the door." By the time he returned to the living room and shrugged out of his jacket, she had his brandy ready for him. He took it and sank down onto the sofa. "Thanks."

"Sure." She settled herself at the other end of the couch and watched as he took a few swallows of his drink. Slowly he began to visibly relax.

After several moments, he leaned back against the cushions. "I guess I needed this."

"Good." She propped her elbow on the top of the couch. "Then are you up to giving me a few answers now?"

He looked over at her, his gaze assessing, as if he were really seeing her for the first time since he'd walked in her door. "I guess it depends on the questions."

"You know the questions *and* the answers, David, and I expect you to give them to me."

The corners of his lips turned up into a half-smile. "Yes, ma'am, Ms. Damaron. Whatever you say, Ms. Damaron."

She chose to let his obvious impersonation of Clifford pass. "I'm very serious, David. A couple of hours ago, you told me that the people who've been shooting at us are after you, not me. I want to know who these people are and how you found out about them."

The half-smile disappeared. "The situation no longer involves you, Kylie. No one is trying to kill you. You're safe. And that's all you need to know."

"You're wrong. In fact, you couldn't be more wrong." She was so intent on getting him to answer her questions, she scooted a cushion closer. "To paraphrase your words of last night, those bullets could have killed me just as easily as they could have killed you, and *that's* what gives me the right to know."

His gaze was cool. "I guess I did say something like that, but you have to understand that from this point on, it's a whole new ball game. From now until I get this situation resolved, I'll simply stay away from you and you'll be fine."

"You aren't listening to me. I didn't say I was worried about my safety. I said I wanted answers. You can stay away from me if you like, but only *after* you tell me what is going on."

He rolled the brandy glass between his palms. "Kylie—"

"I deserve to know, David. For twenty-four hours I've been walking around thinking some crazy person out there wanted me dead. Let me tell you, it's not a good feeling."

"I know and I'm sorry. What you've been through is my fault. Last night when I told you I thought you were the target, I believed it. I had just come home after spending months in the Middle East, tying up every possible loose end. It just didn't make sense that I could be the target."

"So you said."

"And it was the truth, or at least as much of the truth as I knew then. I couldn't figure out how I could have any enemies in the States for the simple reason that I've spent so little time here in the last decade."

Given a few minutes, she could probably come up with exactly how much time he'd spent at home, right down to the day, though she hadn't been aware that she could until that very moment. "So what changed from last night, or even since you left the Middle East?"

Gazing down at his brandy, his expression turned somber. "Quite a lot."

"I don't understand."

Once again, he looked over at her. "Are you sure you want to know the truth?"

"Why wouldn't I?"

"Because it deals with harsh realities that most people never have to encounter or even give serious thought to."

"You forget who you're talking to. I've lived with harsh realities since I was five. Stop protecting me, David. I don't need it."

He lightly grazed the side of a knuckle down her cheek. "You could have fooled me. You looked very fragile both last night and this morning."

"I *wasn't* fragile, not then, not now. Last night I was in shock. Given what happened, who wouldn't be? But I came out of it. So tell me what's going on and make it the truth."

"I wouldn't lie to you, Kylie."

"Don't try to kid me, David. You'd lie to me at the drop of a hat if you thought it was in my best interest."

"I suppose that's true."

"There's no supposing about it."

He smiled. "Has it ever occurred to you how well we know each other?"

They did know each other extremely well, but in the mood she was in, it didn't seem a cause for celebration. "Why in the world wouldn't we? Any two people who've known each other as long as we have certainly should know more than a *few* things about each other."

"Not necessarily."

"You're stalling, David."

He exhaled heavily. "No, actually I wasn't, but okay. You want the truth, I'll give it to you."

He turned sideways on the couch to face her. Last night he'd sat the same way as they'd talked, but tonight would be different. Last night she'd been thrown off balance by the idea that someone had tried to kill her. Maybe she even *had* felt a bit fragile. But she hadn't been frightened for herself, not really.

Yes, she'd been the one who had been shot at. But in the past, if one of her cousins was shot at, it usually meant that someone had declared open season on her entire family. At the time she believed she was the target, and that could have had no other significance than that she'd been the one they'd been able to get to first.

Last night she'd been frightened for her family, and in his own way, David had taken care of her. Tonight, she sensed, he needed her to take care of him. Not that he'd admit it.

"Okay, Kylie, here's your truth. Quite a while ago, my organization discovered a small but alarmingly fanatical group in the Middle East led by a man named Malik Asad. Their goal was to slip into the United States and, through terroristic acts, wreck havoc with our communications and transportation systems, and therefore our government. They had to be stopped as soon as possible and Scott and I were called to head up the job." He swallowed more of the brandy.

She nodded. "Okay, but you must have accomplished your mission, because you said you had tied up everything over there."

"Yeah, it took some doing, but we finally did it. We wiped out the entire group, including Asad. But what we hadn't counted on, and what we didn't know until today, is that there is a cell of Asad's group already over here, in place and ready to go. They're younger than the original group and even more fanatical, if that's possible. This group is led by Asad's son, Hassan."

"Why didn't you know about them?"

"My organization doesn't operate within the boundaries of the United States. Our purpose is to keep possible danger from getting into the country in the first place. That means we focus our intelligence gathering outside the U.S., mainly on countries we believe are encouraging or harboring terrorists."

"So then how did you find out about this cell? And so fast?"

"It wasn't as fast as it should have been." A muscle jumped in his jaw. "My initial decision that you were the target stole precious hours away from us." He shook his head, clearly disgusted with himself. "But this morning, when I found out that a multilevel investigation conducted during the night had come up empty on anyone wanting you dead, I turned my thinking around."

His hands caught her attention. He was holding the crystal snifter between his palms so tightly, she was afraid it would shatter. She reached over and gently tugged it out of his grasp. She didn't think he even noticed. He was staring at a sculpture across the room, but she knew he wasn't seeing it. His entire concentration was focused on what he was telling her.

"On a hunch, I had our intelligence go back to our original information on Asad and his people, with instructions to dig deeper. They uncovered marriage and birth records for Asad and his cronies. Armed with that information, I called in a favor from the FBI. Their search showed that no one by any of those names had entered the country in the last twenty-five years. So I had our intelligence go a couple of levels deeper to search for the names of the fathers of the women who married into this key group. That's when we struck pay dirt."

"What?" she asked, completely engrossed in what he was saying. It was like a giant puzzle that carried life-and-death rules. If you solved it, you lived. If you didn't, you died.

"It turns out that the majority of the members of this newly identified cell were brought over here by their mothers while they were still fairly young. Asad wanted them to grow up and be educated here and to learn Western ways."

"What kind of man would come up with a plan that

long ago that would involve denying himself his wife and son?"

"A fanatical man with hate where his heart should be. Sacrifice means nothing to that type person. And in Asad's case, he knew that one day he'd have a giant payoff—a cell of young men here, in place, and ready to go into action whenever he said the word. They might have adopted certain American customs—the things most kids love, like movies, rock 'n' roll, cars—I don't know. But in private they were still hand-fed the hard-core fanaticism that Asad funneled to them through their mothers."

"David, you can't blame yourself for not thinking of this possibility sooner."

He looked over at her. "It's my job."

"Up until the shooting last night, this group has had no substance or form. How could you have been expected to think of Hassan and his men if you didn't even know they existed? But you did think of them, and relatively quickly too."

"You know what's really interesting?" he said thoughtfully. "It was a brilliant plan. The mothers entered the country with their sons, using the name they'd had before they were married. They claimed to be widows, and everything official, including registering their sons for school, was done under their maiden names."

"It sounds as if it worked superbly."

"It definitely did. There was no way the sons could be connected to their fathers with a routine check. And really, there was no reason to check them out at all. Since they've been here, they've caused zero trouble.

They've lived very quietly, in small, well-kept homes, and blended in with the Muslim community. Hassan and a couple of others attended NYU. Brilliant," he said again. "But in the end, Asad didn't activate them as planned. His death did. And now the sons' anger over the deaths of their fathers and relatives has turned them into full-fledged zealots. They're ready to fight, and we've been left scrambling for information about them."

"But it sounds as if you've been able to come up with quite a bit."

"Only what a computer can show us—where they were living, school records, that sort of thing—and the FBI has helped us out by interviewing neighbors and teachers. But we could fill volumes with what we *don't* know about them." He exhaled a long breath. "It's imperative that we fill in the blanks, and it's going to be damn hard because they've gone underground."

"How do you know that?"

"Their addresses were checked out. No one was home. The mailboxes were stuffed with junk mail. Houseplants were dry and dying. Dirty dishes were in the sinks and had been there for a while. All signs point to the fact that they hurriedly packed and left. We wiped out Asad and his group three weeks ago. That means they've had that long to put their plans into actions. We know they're here, and we've got to find them. But *damn*, it's doing to be tough."

He stood and began to restlessly pace around the room. "Not only do we not know where they are, but we don't know how much financial backing they have, or what their arsenal consists of, or even how many there are of them."

"So," she said, speaking slowly as she tried to see if she could make all the puzzle pieces fit, "it was members of this newly activated group who shot at us both last night and tonight."

"That's right."

"But last night you said you'd been standing out there by the car for thirty minutes, yet they didn't start shooting at you until I came out."

He grimaced. "The timing appears to be a fluke. Remember, I'd only been home less than twenty-four hours. They couldn't have known exactly when I would be flying in, so they were scrambling for information about me, much as I'm now scrambling for information about them. But somewhere along the line we speculate they picked up my scent and put some sort of loose tail on me to get an idea of my schedule while they formed their plans.

"Up until the restaurant, they were still in the planning stages of how to get me. They hadn't expected to find me out in the open like I was, like a damn sitting duck. The guy who found me must have put in a call to Hassan. If Hassan had been two minutes later in marshaling his men and hightailing it over to the restaurant, they would have missed us."

She spread her hands. "But isn't that good news? They can't be too dangerous if it took them that long to react."

"Last night wasn't planned. Tonight was."

"How?"

"I let my guard down." He shook his head again. "I

can't believe how stupid I've been. I called Tim late this afternoon on my cell phone to find out which stores were going to stay open for us. He read me the list and I named the stores I was interested in. There were only three. You said you felt as if someone were watching you at the store you'd just come from. That store was on my list, but at the last minute I decided to skip it and go to my last choice, mainly because I called Tim again and found out that's where you were."

"You were there to see me?"

He nodded. "I wanted to let you know as soon as possible that you weren't the target." He shook his head in self-disgust. "It's clear now they found my cell's frequency and listened in on my calls. You said you also felt that you were being watched in the second-to-the-last store you were at. Knowing that, we figure they sent teams into the last two stores on my list before they closed, and had them hide and wait for me to show up. Somehow they got by all the security. The first team's wait was futile, because I decided to skip that store. The second team struck gold."

"Was that second team killed?" she asked, realizing with a start that she didn't know. Tim and David had hustled her out of the store so quickly she hadn't seen any bodies.

"Yes."

"What about the team at the other store?"

"They were gone by the time Tim had it checked out."

She stared at him, going back over all the information he'd given her, and she realized he'd left out one very vital piece of information. "Why *you*, David? Why do they specifically want to kill you? Or is your friend Scott also included in their plans?"

He shook his head. "From the bits and pieces of information that're coming in now, we've been able to figure out that, for now, it's only me they want. *I* was the one who killed Asad, and because I did, I've become the most important focus for his son. Hassan's vowed to avenge his father's death by killing his killer—me."

A chill shivered through her and she automatically glanced over at the still-burning fire. As far as she could tell, it was doing a good job of throwing heat out into the room. She hugged herself, trying to counteract the incomprehensible chill she felt. "And that's why the guy who had tailed you to the restaurant last night didn't try to kill you himself?"

"Right. It would have been a relatively easy kill for him, but he didn't even take a shot. Because he didn't, and because we've seen this same thing in other cases, we've been able to deduce that, with Hassan, it's all about order. We're very confident that in his mind, he must be the one to kill me and he must do it *first*, before any of his men who lost fathers or uncles in the raid three weeks ago can seek revenge."

"But that's crazy."

He cut his gaze to her. "Who said he was sane?"

"Right." She felt even colder than she had a moment ago. "Okay. Now I understand why you told Tim that your organization would take over this morning. But you know, this is not all bad news. Now all you have to do is stay out of sight until they're located and caught. Right?"

"That would be one approach," he said without expression.

She was barely able to stifle a groan. "Let me guess. It's not the approach you've chosen."

He nodded. "Finding Hassan and his group and neutralizing them is of paramount importance. They're simply too dangerous. They can't be allowed to run around unchecked for any longer than is necessary. The damage they are capable of can't even be calculated. They could take a busload of kids hostage and kill one every hour on the hour until I turn myself over to them. They could do the same thing with an office building, where even more people would be killed. Plus, as long as I'm their number one target, the people around me are in danger. As you pointed out before, you could have easily been killed last night or tonight. I can't sit here in the Tower and do nothing."

No, she thought, that wouldn't be his style. He was a man of action, accustomed to the worst of mankind and the stark realities of death. Even as he talked about Hassan and his group, she'd sensed the adrenaline and energy as his body readied itself for battle. She even believed he was looking forward to it.

But it was her worst nightmare come to life.

"So what's your next step?" she asked, managing to keep her voice calm.

"I'm going to get a couple of hours' sleep, then meet Scott in the morning for a strategy session."

"To figure out how to find the group?"

"Actually, we don't have enough information on them yet to find them, but then we don't need to."

She froze. "You're going to use yourself as bait, aren't you?"

Slipping his hands into the pockets of his slacks, he walked over to look at a new painting she'd recently acquired. "It's the quickest way."

The air went out of her body. She'd done everything to protect herself from just this kind of sequence of events, which would invariably end when someone would come and tell her that David had been killed. But in the end, nothing had worked for her—not even their seven-year estrangement.

And this time the violence he was facing wasn't in some foreign country, but in the city where she lived—in fact, right in front of her eyes.

She jumped up from the sofa and began to do some of her own pacing. Twice now David had been lucky enough to escape his assassin's bullets. The third time might prove to be Hassan's charm, and David planned to give her no alternative but to watch and wait until Hassan killed him.

But she wasn't strong enough to watch him die. She *wasn't*. If anything happened to him, she couldn't even begin to imagine how dark her world would become. She came to a halt.

She'd done it, she reflected. She couldn't quite believe it, but it was true. She'd just admitted to herself how important David was to her. How important he'd always been. How important he would always be. And she'd be damned if she would sit silently by and watch him go out and get himself killed.

She turned toward him and found him watching her. She cleared her throat. "So let me get this straight.

You're going to paint a big, fat target on yourself and walk around until they shoot you. Can you possibly think of anything more *stupid*, David?"

He turned away from the painting with a slight smile. "My scenario has a slightly different ending than the one you're thinking of. In mine, I don't get shot."

"Oh, right. What are the odds? One in a million?"

"That's what I love to hear," he said dryly. "Optimism."

"Give me something to be optimistic about."

"Look, Kylie. You're forgetting that I'll have backup. Also the FBI is in on this now, and they're offering all the help we want."

"And that should make me feel better?" She shook her head. "I'm not forgetting anything, David. You said yourself that this group is fanatical. That means they're willing to *die* to achieve their goals. Two of their group did just that tonight. People who are willing to die can't be guarded against. You can't predict what they'll do, which means that you can't plan against them. For goodness' sakes, David, I shouldn't have to be telling you this. You should know it."

"I do."

She watched as he moved around the room. "That's all you've got to say?" she asked incredulously.

"There's really nothing else *to* say. Your assessment is one hundred percent correct. The deaths in the Middle East, added to the two tonight, will shorten Hassan's already shortened fuse and he'll come after me with everything he's got.

He paused, thinking. "You know, it's interesting. If he considered the situation before him in a rational manner, he would have a much better success rate for his group. If he'd simply forget about me and go ahead with their original terroristic plans, there'd be nothing we could do about it. We're totally in the dark about this group's plans."

"It's certainly too bad Hassan doesn't have you for an advisor, isn't it?"

He shrugged. "Looking at it from that viewpoint, I'm actually grateful he's going to come after me first, because he'll expose himself, and if we're lucky—"

Her breath caught in her chest. "If you're *lucky?* You're depending on *luck?*"

His gaze was somber. "You wanted the truth, Kylie. There's no way I can sugarcoat this situation. No matter how you look at it, it's grim."

Her heart rate had kicked into high gear. She crossed to him and looked straight into his eyes. "Tell me something, David. What is it about you that makes you want to constantly put yourself in the path of danger? Most people—most *sane* people—go out of their way to avoid it. But *you* . . . you walk right into it, willingly and knowingly."

He eyed her thoughtfully. "If a person didn't know any better, Kylie, he would almost think you care about me."

Throwing up her hands, she spun away. She was so angry and frustrated that she wasn't sure she could even think straight. She made her way to the window and absently noticed that it had started to snow again. A white Christmas seemed a sure thing now. God, what was she going to do about David?

Gently she touched the pane, relishing its cool feel.

"Of course I care," she said carefully, her voice quieter. "Why wouldn't I? You've been in my life for as long as I can remember."

"And that's the only reason?"

"What other reason could there be?"

"I could think of a couple."

Slowly he walked up behind her and laid his hand over hers. His body brushed against hers from the back. The coolness seeped from her hand and was replaced by heat, the same heat that had begun to circulate through her.

She pulled her hand from beneath his and moved away from him. Grabbing a pillow, she hugged it against her chest as she collapsed onto the sofa. She was handling the situation just as badly as she always knew she would, she thought ruefully. "Why did you even bother to come home? If you were going to get killed anyway, why didn't you simply stay over there and be done with it?"

He leaned back against the window and gazed at her. "Because, Kylie—and please try to remember this—I don't plan to get killed."

"You sure could have fooled me with that imbecilic idea of yours."

He strolled to a chair near her, propped his hips against the chair's arm, and stretched his long legs out in front of him. "You're angry with me, Kylie, and I understand why. But I need to tell you that if you keep going the way you're going, you'll lead us straight into a full-blown argument." He cocked his head to one side and regarded her, a gentle smile in his eyes. "Is that what you want? Do you want to pick a fight with me tonight so that maybe tomorrow, if I'm killed, you won't care so much?"

She gasped. "What a preposterous thing to say."

"Is it?"

She didn't know if he was right or wrong and she wasn't sure she wanted to know. All she really wanted to do was shake some sense into him. But deep down, she knew that his mind wouldn't, couldn't, be changed, not by her or by anyone. And the riskiest thing she could do right now would be to continue to poke and prod at him until he got angry. She could handle her own anger, but she wasn't sure she could handle his, not when his tomorrow was so uncertain. She didn't want their last words to each other to be harsh.

"No, I don't want to fight with you," she said slowly, trying to think how she wanted to proceed. "That's not my intention at all. Just please do me a favor and rethink using yourself for bait. I mean, where is it written that you have to be the one to save the world this time?"

"Another good question." Standing, he reached out his arm, clasped her hand, and drew her to her feet.

Her forehead wrinkled as she looked up at him. "What are you doing?"

"Trying to get you closer to me," he said, running a finger along the shoulder of her robe. "A minute ago, you also asked me why I even bothered to come home. Do you still want to know?"

She swallowed. "Yes."

"Then, Kylie, pick which question you'd like me to answer first."

EIGHT

Something had changed. David's voice had become softer, but strangely the angles of his face had become sharper.

"Okay," Kylie said, any lingering anger giving over to a new wariness. "Let's start with why it has to be you."

"Because I'm the only one it *can* be."

"Not if you do it the more reasonable way."

"And what's that?" He gently ran his fingers up the back of her neck and into her hair. "Stay here in the Tower until enough information is gathered on the group that they can be taken out?" He shook his head. "No, Kylie. Too many lives could be lost before that happened."

"You don't know that for sure," she said suddenly, feeling as if she were on the brink of tears. She blinked away any suspicious moistness in her eyes.

"As a matter of fact, I do."

"You can't possibly be that confident that you're right on this."

"I'm afraid that I can guarantee you that I am."

She knew she wasn't gaining any ground. Truthfully, the fight had been lost even before she'd started it. But she had to keep trying, because she continued to have an overpowering sensation that after tonight, she might not see him alive again. She prayed with all her heart she was wrong. But what if she wasn't?

He waited for several moments, gazing down at her. "Any more comments on that particular subject?" With his fingers beneath the lapels, he arranged the robe around her, seemingly to suit himself.

She tried to stop his distracting movements by folding her arms. "How can there be, when you won't even consider that I could be right?"

"I'm sorry, Kylie," he said, his voice going even softer, "but I'm afraid you can't win on that particular subject. So, shall we go on to the next question? The one that has to do with why I came home?"

She was having trouble thinking straight when he was standing so near to her and continuing to do things with the lapels that lay over her breasts. She backed away from his touch and went to stand by the fireplace. "It was a sarcastic question, as I'm sure you know. Besides, you already told me. Your mother likes you home for Christmas. Also, you thought you'd completed your mission."

Suddenly his gaze sharpened, as if, she thought oddly, he were trying to decide what to tell her. She heard the fire crackle in the fireplace and felt heat soak through her robe and gown to warm her bare skin. And she didn't know why, but it seemed as if the floor beneath her had shifted. Or maybe it was something about David's mood that had changed.

One thing she knew, though. At least part of the heat she was feeling was coming from David. No matter the situation or the subject, he always radiated a heated masculinity. Except this time it was more than that. This time there was a new intensity about him, an intensity that left her at once puzzled and weak in the knees.

"Both of those reasons are true," he said slowly, "but I had an even stronger motive to come home."

"What?"

"You."

She went still. "I'm afraid I don't understand."

"Then I'll make myself clearer. I came home to try to straighten out what happened between us years ago."

The shock of his answer stole the heat from her body and thought from her mind, which was why she was so surprised to hear herself speak. "I think seven years of silence on both of our parts means there's nothing to say."

"If you'll recall, I *tried* to break the silence between us the first couple of years. But each time you were with someone new, and you gave me the distinct impression that you didn't want to talk about it or have anything to do with me."

She threaded her fingers together. "Actually, now that you've brought it up, your impression was right. What's more, scraping up that particular memory doesn't appeal to me in the least. But"—she looked down at her fingers, then raised her face to meet his gaze—"I realize now that I acted less than gracious to you and I'm sorry about that. I just felt it would be better for both of us to move on to the next stage of our lives."

"To hell with gracious! Tell me why you felt it better for us to move on."

"Because . . ." She swallowed, still having trouble thinking. "Just because."

He gave a short, hard laugh that cut through the air and scraped against her skin. "Come on, Kylie. I *know* you can do better than that."

She shrugged and looked away. "As I just said, I'd rather not relive that night."

"Tough. I *do.*"

She jerked her hands apart and stuffed them into the deep pockets of her robe. It was better than slapping him. She didn't *want* to remember that time. What was the point? Particularly when it would come stacked atop the Hassan crisis David would be facing tomorrow? "For goodness' sakes, *why?*"

His expression hardened and so did his voice. "Because *I* decided it was time. Because you still feel something for me and you can't deny it. And even if you did, your response to my kiss last night would prove you wrong. And because I still feel something for you or I wouldn't have bothered to kiss you in the first place."

Kylie was barely able to prevent her mouth from dropping open. At that moment, there was so much electricity and heat in the room, she wouldn't have been surprised to see small fires spark to life in the air around them. But it didn't matter. She didn't want to talk about the two of them. She hadn't even had time to consider her earlier realization that she still cared deeply for him.

She edged away from him and the fireplace. "We've gotten totally off the subject, David."

"Not as far as I'm concerned."

"The subject was, *is*, that someone is trying to kill you."

"So what else is new?"

Inside the robe's pockets, her hands balled into fists. "Damn you, David! Why are you so cavalier about your life?"

His gaze was hard and unyielding. "I'll tell you what, Kylie. Tomorrow I'll worry about my life, but for tonight I want to talk about you and me."

She closed her eyes and shook her head. Talking about the past would solve nothing. Even though she'd admitted to herself that her reaction after their night together and the intervening seven years had been her fault, not his, nothing had changed. He still worked in one of the most dangerous professions in the world, and she'd still never been able to come to a resolution about the fear that had kept her from seeking him out before now.

"Listen to me, David. There *is* no you and me. And even if there were, tomorrow you're determined to go out and make yourself a target, which will most likely end with you being killed. Then I would be left alone. *Again.*" Did he flinch? For a moment it looked as if he did. Maybe she was finally getting through to him. Unfortunately, his next words disabused her of that notion.

"Yeah, you're right. Or I could be run over by a truck. Or a crate could fall on me. Or one of those things could even happen to you. But you know what, Kylie? If one of those things did happen, we'd at least have tonight together."

Harsh, hurtful words and confused thoughts hung in the air between them, as silence pulsated in the around them.

"I can't live like that, David."

"You do it every day. It's called being alive, and it's also part of being a Damaron."

"My cousins and I may make high-profile targets, but my life is nowhere near as hazardous as yours. No one's is. We control the danger so that its chance at us is minimal."

"Who are you kidding? Danger can't be controlled. Didn't the last two nights show you that?"

"I don't go out looking for danger, David! You do, and it's *crazy*. Absolutely *crazy*."

He opened his mouth to retort, then, to her surprise, seemed to catch himself. Never once dropping his gaze from her, he took several calming breaths. "Tell me something. What happened to that brave Kylie I used to know? The one who so fearlessly told me to meet her in the studio that night?"

"She vanished under a mound of realism when she woke up alone the next morning."

He stared at her for several moments. And as she met his gaze, she had no idea what he'd say or do next. For all she knew, he might stalk out the door. He might also stay and fight with her some more. As badly as she hated fighting with him, she was still hoping for the latter. As long as he was with her, he wasn't out on the street offering himself as a target.

"Okay," he said. "Let's talk about that morning. In retrospect, leaving like I did was a lousy thing to do, but Kylie, you knew what I did for a living. Over the years, there have been countless times when you've seen me have to get up and leave, no matter what else was going on. And besides, it wasn't like you woke up the next morning and thought you'd never see me again."

And what if she had thought that? She rubbed her arms, then folded them around her waist. All of a sudden she didn't want to argue with him anymore. Her strength was deserting her. Maybe if they both had a good night's sleep they'd have clearer heads in the morning. Then she could intercept him before he had a chance to leave, and talk to him again. "Look, I'm sorry I even mentioned how you left." She turned her wrist to glance at her watch. "Didn't you say you were tired?"

"Not anymore." Suddenly he grabbed her arm and led her over to the sofa, where he pulled her down beside him.

"What are you doing?"

"I'm trying to have a conversation with you without having to follow you all over the room."

"Didn't anyone ever tell you that you can't always have what you want?"

"Yeah," he said, without releasing her arm. "The Rolling Stones, but I didn't believe them. So tell me— what bothered you the most about those hours we spent together? The fact that I took your virginity?

Believe me, no one was more surprised than I was. For years, I'd seen the way guys flocked to you. I didn't like to think about it—in fact, I hated it—but it seemed only natural that you'd fall for at least one of them." His gaze and voice softened. "But *I* was the first, just as if it were meant to be, and believe me, it didn't bother me one damned bit."

His words were penetrating, puncturing her defenses with his truth. She tried to pull her wrist from his hand, but he simply tightened his hold, not enough to hurt her, but enough to keep her where she was. She fell back on the only defense she had left. Words. "That you were the first meant nothing more than the fact that I'd had too much champagne."

Incredibly he smiled. "Sorry, Kylie, but I don't buy it. Remember, I was there that night when the two of us nearly went up in flames. Was it that part that bothered you? Or was it really about what you said before— that I left without waking you? Because if it was, I apologize profusely. Believe me, I hated like hell doing that, but as hard as it was to leave you sleeping, it would have been impossible if you'd been awake. I would have had to make love to you again and I couldn't afford the time."

She jerked her wrist free. She knew they were getting far off their original subject, but he was getting to her in a really big way. "So you're saying that because of sex, I had to wake up alone with only a note that said virtually nothing?"

"I said I'd contact you when I could, which I did."

"Eight months later."

"Damn it, Kylie! Don't you think it was hard on me

too? It was sheer hell. I'm used to that particular territory because that's where I work. But even so, missing you took me to a new and different level of hell and it damn near did me in."

Surprisingly it gave her no satisfaction to hear that he'd hurt too. She gave a shake of her head. Damn him. Why couldn't he simply let the subject drop? But whatever his reason, she couldn't continue sitting so close to him. She rose and he didn't try to stop her as she moved away. Her hands clenched, then opened again. She'd told him much more than she ever planned to about her reaction to what he'd done, but he'd brought the subject up and her words had just come tumbling out.

"Just out of curiosity, what did you do with the sapphire necklace I left you?"

"I put it in my safe."

"Have you ever worn it?"

"No."

"It seems that nothing I did then pleased you. Except that I distinctly remember you quivering beneath my hands with unadulterated ecstasy."

She whirled on him. "Stop it, David. You're being deliberately cruel."

"What I'm being, Kylie, is deliberately *truthful*."

"God, David, what's the use of rehashing all of this?"

He surged to his feet, and before she realized what he was going to do, he was at her side, his eyes glittering hotly. "Because I *still* want you. And because I know that before I can have you again, I have to get through all the barriers you've erected against me in the last seven years."

"Before you can have me again?" she said, her trembling voice rising. "This is still all about *sex?*"

Something changed in him. He didn't move, but she saw him deliberately pull back on the force of his words and emotions.

"You tell me, Kylie," he said, his voice quiet again. "Was it only about sex when you invited me to your studio?"

If she'd answered him, she would have had to say that at the time she was sure it was love. Whatever happened that night had been building for quite some time. But telling him that would leave her much too vulnerable.

He casually slipped his hands into his pants pockets. "There seems to be nothing we can agree on tonight. Of course, it doesn't help that you have a conveniently cloudy memory, does it? But if you would ever allow yourself to be truthful, you'd have to agree that what happened that night between us was fantastic. And you'd also have to agree that if we gave ourselves another chance, we could have nights far more incredible than that one."

She couldn't deny anything he'd just said, not even the last part. She'd long ago admitted to herself that she'd been a coward by trying to block him from her life the last seven years. Now she had to admit that she was afraid to want him again, afraid of the pain that would certainly come when he left once more. Or when he was killed. "Time passes, David. Things change."

"That's true enough," he said calmly. "But then some things *never* change."

He reached for her, and holding her gaze with his and taking his time, he drew her to him. Then, just as slowly, he brought his lips down on hers, lightly, confidently. Last night his kiss had been an electric shock that had caught her off guard and had left her no time to brace herself or throw up any barrier. Tonight he'd gone slowly, giving her time to realize what he was about to do, and still she hadn't been successful in guarding herself. In fact, she hadn't even tried.

She'd *wanted* this. She'd wanted it more than she wanted to be safe. How incredibly stupid of her, she thought, just as she gave in to the spell of his kiss.

Gradually he increased the pressure of his mouth and automatically her lips parted. With a husky groan, his tongue swept in and took command with hard, sexual thrusts that sent thrills zooming down to her toes. But then in the next moment, he switched to sensitive, teasing strokes that had her heart fluttering and warmth sliding through her. It was enough to undo her.

At the same time, he gently caressed her face, just as he used to do when she young. But she was an adult now, an adult who wasn't supposed to be afraid anymore, and who now reacted to his caresses quite differently. When he stroked her skin, she felt as if his fingers were made of fire and each touch lit small flames throughout her body.

Barely aware of what she was doing, she moved closer, pressing herself against him, softening her body to adjust to the masculine muscle and bone of him. A river of hot sweetness was running through her and she called herself crazy.

But suddenly it was all so easy, as if her body had maintained a memory of how it had been between the two of them seven years ago, and she flowed into him just as she had on that night. In some secret recess of her heart, she'd known her reaction to him would be like this. She'd known her wanting would be even stronger and more urgent than it had been on the night of her birthday party. It was as if those intervening years hadn't happened at all, and neither had the painful lessons she'd learned. She wanted him with everything that was in her—exactly what she'd been so afraid of for so long.

She raised her hands to either side of his face and pulled him closer to her, urging him to kiss her harder. But no matter how much she silently entreated, he wouldn't hurry his kisses or his touches. He continued kissing her slowly, deeply, sensually. It felt as if he were savoring each and every taste of her. But more than that, it felt as if he were attempting to pull her soul from her body and into his.

He was hard against her, his desire for her pulsating, matching the aching throb inside her. Her body was preparing for him, growing moist and even more malleable, and she had no control over it.

But he did, she thought hazily. He knew exactly what his scorching-hot kisses and gentle touches were doing to her. He was an expert and he was making her want him until she was close to being crazed with need. In fact, she was an inch away from allowing herself to be mindlessly seduced, and God help her, that was exactly what she wanted. If she did and said nothing, they'd be in her bed in the next minute, undressing each other.

And as much as she wanted that, she also knew it was crucial that she think through what was about to happen between them. She was older now, wiser, and she knew how important it was that she be very, very sure not only that this was what she wanted to do, but that she could handle whatever the aftermath might be. She hadn't gone through the last seven years for nothing. Making love wouldn't automatically make everything better between them. It wasn't that simple— nothing was.

No. She had to know that afterward she could be brave enough and strong enough to let him go and then deal with the heartache she knew would follow. And she didn't know that. Not yet, and maybe not ever. With a sound of anguish, she pushed him away.

Her chest hurt as she tried to breathe while the desire she saw in his eyes made her weak. But she met his gaze unflinchingly. She wanted to ask him for understanding, but she honestly didn't know what to tell him to make him understand.

"You know what, Kylie?" he asked, his voice hoarse and gruff. "Maybe you're right. Maybe I will be killed tomorrow, and if that happens, what will make you feel better? Having me say goodnight right now and go across the hall to my own bed? Or having me stay and make love to you?" He reached out and spread his hand along her jawline to cup her face. "Tell me which memory will comfort you best when, according to you, the inevitable happens and the news comes that I've been gunned down in the street."

Fresh anger sprang from nowhere and she slapped his hand away. "If you think for one minute that a few hours of rolling around on the bed with you would make me feel better if you died, then you're very much mistaken."

His eyes gleamed with a puzzling satisfaction. "You're right," he said softly. "There's not a thing in the world that could comfort someone if the person she loves dies."

"I didn't say—"

"Ssshh." He took a step closer. "For a few hours, put aside your fears and *live* with me. What's important is that we're here, right now, together. Despite what happened seven years ago, you want me, and I sure as hell want you."

She felt herself sway toward him and reached for something that would snap her out of it. "Does this approach usually work well for you? The one out of those old war movies where the guy is telling the girl that he'll be leaving for the front tomorrow and they may only have the one night together?"

He gave her an oddly sweet, sad smile. "So you won't even try for me."

She shook her head. "Try what?"

"To believe with all your heart that I won't be killed tomorrow. Then once you manage that, try believing I won't be killed the next day, then the day after that one. Before you know it, you'll be brave enough to forget the past and look toward the future."

Her eyes filled with tears. "That's what I was doing when I invited you to the studio."

"Kylie, you asked why I came home. I came home to tell you I still care very much for you and to try to win you back. I can't even begin to say how sorry I am that somehow, in some way, I hurt you back then. But I was hurt pretty badly too. In fact I threw myself back into my work to try to forget you. I became an adrenaline junkie, but it didn't help. Nothing did. So here I am, asking you to forget the past and give us another chance."

A tear spilled out of one eye and rolled down her face. "But why now? Why not two or four or six years ago? What's so different about this year?"

"I'm not sure I can tell you exactly, but I do know that I received a definite wake-up call. When I learned you were seeing Molinari, I panicked. I suddenly realized I didn't want to lose you—not to Molinari, not to any other man."

"That's very territorial of you," she said, shaken. "What gives you the right?"

"Hell, Kylie, I don't know," He flung out a hand. "Maybe you gave it to me when you were five and first ran across that hall and into my arms. Or maybe I decided you were going to be mine when you were sixteen and first batted those long lashes of yours at me." He ran his hand around the back of his neck. "The truth is, no matter what your age has been, you've never been out of my mind. *Never*. In one way or another, I think I've always considered you mine."

His words shook her as she remembered the proprietary feelings she'd always had for him, right up until she woke up the morning after her twenty-first birthday party.

He exhaled. "Look, you've been through a lot in the last couple of days. In fact, you're probably running on little more than nerves. But think about what I've said, because believe me, I'm not through trying to get you back. Not by a long shot." He leaned down and pressed a soft kiss to her lips that gave a new burst of life to the heat that still simmered in her veins. "Sleep well," he whispered, then he turned and headed toward the door.

She watched him, her pulse beating rapidly. He was going to walk straight out her door tonight and into the crosshairs of a gun tomorrow, she thought, her heart aching for him.

He knew all about danger, and he understood it would be stalking him at dawn tomorrow. He courted danger. He danced with it. And up until now, he'd always outwitted it. But something kept telling her that this time the danger might win.

Even an amateur like herself knew the odds were against him, and though he wouldn't admit it to her, he knew it too. Yet he would still go out tomorrow because it was his job and because he considered the responsibility his.

He didn't care about himself, but she did. She cared more than she could say.

"Wait."

NINE

David turned back. "What is it?"

"Stay. Please . . . stay."

His body stiffened. "Are you sure?"

Kylie nodded. "Absolutely." They'd said a lot to each other in the past couple of hours—maybe too much, maybe not enough. But together, she and David had survived two violent attacks in the last twenty-four hours, and during that time they had talked more than in the whole seven years they'd been estranged.

And she'd learned something very important tonight. Nothing made a person live in the present more than danger, and before this situation with Hassan was over, there would certainly be more danger. Under such circumstances, how could she allow the past to continue to be important to her? And how could she allow her fears to stand in the way of something they both wanted so badly? Tonight might be their only chance to show each other how much they cared.

"You better be sure," he said, his voice rough, his gaze fixed steadily on her, "because I'm not going to ask you again."

"I'm sure." *She loved him.* Before tonight she would have been surprised at the acknowledgment. But after all her agonizing, all her rationalizations, it had come down to one simple fact. She'd always loved him and always would, and there was nothing she could do about it.

Her only doubt now was about herself and whether she could keep her heart in one piece afterward. Instinctively she knew she'd never again be able to build a barrier against him, but then, what did it matter? At the moment tomorrow seemed a long way away. She'd deal with it when it came.

David walked slowly toward her, his gaze burning with fire. When he got within arm's length of her, he stopped. "You should know that you're never going to get away from me again."

She smiled up at him. "I have no plans to go anywhere."

With a groan, he pulled her to him and brought his mouth down on hers, crushing her lips with his, hard, hot, and demanding. If she'd had any remaining doubts, they would have quickly disintegrated beneath the heat that instantly took possession of her, but she had none. And it felt right, so right—the two of them together again. Tonight and always, she silently prayed. *Always.*

Standing on tiptoe, she returned his kiss fully and without restriction, slipping her arms around his neck and her fingers up into his hair, stripping off the tie until his hair fell loose around his face.

Her blood ran hot; her body turned soft. She murmured something, or at least she thought she did. She wasn't sure what she'd said or if he'd heard her, but the meaning, if not the words, got through to him.

Thankfully, he must have felt the same way, because with a rough groan, he tore his lips from hers. "I've got to get you to a bed before I explode."

While her body burned and her mind still reeled with feelings both new and old, he swept her up into his arms and carried her into her bedroom. There, he placed her on the satin comforter that covered her bed, then quickly undressed.

She'd left a bedside lamp on and it cast a golden glow over them. She had the vague notion that she should probably get up and pull back the comforter. She should also probably undress, but she couldn't tear her eyes away from David.

He skimmed his sweater over his head, baring his muscled arms and broad chest. He was beautiful, she thought. His skin gleamed beneath the light, and dark, curling hair covered his chest, then narrowed down to disappear beneath his belt. His nipples were small and dark and her hands itched to trace the small circles around them.

She held her arms up to him. "Come to bed."

He hesitated, then, with a grin that held more agony than humor, resumed undressing, stripping off his belt and dropping it to the carpet. "Don't, Kylie. Or I'll take you while we're both still dressed."

"Clothes don't matter."

He made a sound somewhere between a groan and a laugh. "You're undermining all my good intentions." He stripped off his belt and let it fall to the carpet, then unzipped his pants.

"And how am I doing?"

The heat in his eyes scorched through her robe and gown to her skin, to her blood, to her heart. "If you were doing any better, I'd be a fumbling idiot."

"I just want to feel you inside me, David. It's been so long . . ."

"Oh, God, Kylie." Hastily he pushed the pants down his thighs and stepped out of them, just as a moment later he shed his briefs.

Then he straightened, towering above her, and she saw that his whole body was a mass of muscles, his arousal strong and pulsing. As small as she was, if he'd been anyone else, she might have been afraid of him. But he'd never once hurt her physically, not in the heat of lovemaking, or in the careless fun of play, or in the fury of anger, and she certainly wasn't afraid of him now.

In fact, tremors of anticipation shook her. She ached to touch him, to taste him, to feel him against her, inside her. It seemed like an eternity since they'd made love. And yes, she thought. For him it might have been sex, but for her it had been lovemaking.

"I'm starved for you," he said hoarsely and came down on the bed and stretched out beside her.

Drawing in a deep breath, Kylie inhaled his darkly erotic scent, which mingled with the perfumed air of her bedroom. "I'm starved for you too," she whispered, reaching up to touch his face.

A shudder raked his body. "Why in hell did we wait so long?"

She silently echoed his question. At this precise moment it seemed incomprehensible that they had waited so long and denied themselves such pleasure. She accepted the guilt, but now that she was in his arms again, she didn't want to think about anything else but him and the next few hours.

And he didn't even give her a chance to answer. He kissed her, hungrily, possessively, with the determination of a man reclaiming what was once his. Beneath the onslaught of his passion, she responded, surrendering completely to him as her mouth opened beneath his and her tongue thrust upward to meet his.

Her body ached as if she had a fever. She could barely think, but then she didn't have to. All that was important was David and their raw, basic need for each other.

Somewhere along the line, the belt of her cashmere robe had come untied. David spread open the robe, revealing the silky nightgown, and placed his hand on her stomach, his fingers easily spanning the narrow width from hipbone to hipbone. Then he clenched his hand, drawing in a large handful of the silk and sending heat shimmering over her nerves.

Unwilling to wait a moment longer for the ultimate satisfaction that was so near, she broke off the kiss and tried to push his hand away. "Let me undress," she whispered.

He gave a husky laugh. "A minute ago, clothes didn't matter."

"A minute ago, I didn't have you naked beside me. I want to feel your skin against mine."

There'd been a drought in her life since they'd last made love, she realized, and being this close to him again, talking to him, touching him, was almost overwhelming to her. Sensations and feelings layered over more sensations and feelings. All good, all miraculous.

He pulled the gown up along her thighs, then she raised her hips so that he could lift the gown above her breasts. She moved again, expecting him to strip the gown over her head, but the sight of her nearly naked body momentarily stilled him.

With a rough sound, he bent his head and drew her nipple into his mouth, causing her stomach to contract with heated desire. Continuing to suckle deeply, he slowly, expertly caressed and kneaded the other breast. A deep-seated pleasure took possession of her. She felt it in her bones, in her belly, between her legs. With a moan, she arched her hips.

"I've always remembered how fantastic making love to you was," he said, his mouth moving over her nipple as he did. "I could never get it out of my mind, but memories can't touch the reality."

"I know," she whispered. Maybe it was the years of constantly repressing her true feelings about him. Or maybe it was as he said, that no matter how strong the memories, years had a tendency to fade them. Whatever the cause, she was unable to endure any more of the exquisite pleasure and she was ready to make new memories. She pushed against his shoulder. "Wait."

Concern filled his eyes. "Am I hurting you?"

She gave a light laugh. "Not at all. It's just that I

want to get rid of what little clothes I'm still wearing so that there'll be no part of you I can't feel."

A husky laugh rumbled up from his chest. He helped her to sit up and pull the gown over her head, then he tossed it aside. "Next time, we'll either stay dressed or completely undress at the beginning." His remark was light, but his voice showed the strain of waiting.

Shifting her hips, she tugged the robe out from under her. "Now," she said, turning back to him with satisfaction, "I can really enjoy touching you."

"What took you so long?" he asked, pulling her down to the bed.

Momentarily she felt the satin comforter caress her skin, but then his arm was around her, drawing her on top of him, and she felt hot skin and hard muscles.

"Go ahead," he whispered. "Touch me. I don't mind at all." His fingers threaded up into her hair. Then, gently but inexorably, he pulled her head downward until her lips met his for another hot, scorching kiss, and before she knew it, the fire and urgency of the kiss had her writhing on top of his body.

Her breasts nestled into the curling texture of his chest hair, and lower, her body encountered the hard length of his sex. Frenzied with passion, she shifted her legs around his arousal, but she couldn't feel its hardness where she really wanted to feel it—inside her.

Then suddenly, as if reading her mind, he cradled her head with his hand and rolled them over so that he was on top of her. "We've wasted seven years," he muttered. "I don't want to waste one more second."

"Neither do I." Fiery emotions clogged her throat and filled her chest and belly. She was more than ready.

David positioned himself between her legs and thrust into her warm, waiting depths. A soft cry escaped her throat as pleasure ripped through her. After so many years, it should have been awkward between them, more difficult for her body to adjust to his, but it wasn't. The immeasurable satisfaction of once again being joined as one was intensely gratifying on a whole other level that she'd never known before. It felt so right, so perfect, as if her body had been empty all these years, but now was filled. Finally, once more, she was whole.

She clutched at his shoulders, his back, his hips, feeling the power of his muscles ripple as he pressed flaming kisses to her throat, face, and lips and continued to stroke in and out of her, each time going deeper. And just when she thought it was impossible, he awakened new pleasures within her, stealing her breath and driving her higher. Waves of heavenly feelings hit her, one after the other, until she was totally engulfed by them.

And while she was clinging to him, he looked down at her, his gaze burning hotly. "Tell me that there hasn't been any man since me," he ordered, his voice thick, his tone fierce. "Tell me that no other man has made love to you but me."

She didn't want to talk. Her senses were too full, her mind too empty. Passion held her in its ever-tightening grip and a powerful tension had begun to coil inside her. In addition, she felt the heat climbing, threatening to engulf and incinerate her.

"Tell me."

"No," she managed. "No man has."

"Is that the truth?" he asked, softer.

"Don't you think my body would feel different to you if I'd been with anyone else?"

A hard shudder trembled through him. He cupped her buttocks and plunged deeper into her. "You're *mine*," he said darkly. "You've *always* been mine and you always will be."

His thrusts became faster. Her tension wound tighter. The pleasure increased, hooked into her with more power. Then all at once, her breath caught and her grip on him tightened. Her nails dug into his back and she arched. David made an indistinguishable sound and drove into her again and again. Then she was climbing, up and up, soaring over the top through a blaze of the most intense ecstasy she'd ever known, and taking David with her.

Spent and quiet, Kylie lay beside David, his arm around her, her head resting on his chest, one of her legs thrown over his. Her breathing had finally slowed, her heartbeat had at last evened. Every breath she took smelled of him, them—their lovemaking, her perfume, their sweat. She'd be content to stay where she was forever, she thought lazily.

"Are you all right?" His words rumbled beneath her ear.

She smiled slightly, her mouth moving against the hairs of his chest. "I'm more than all right."

"Good." He hugged her against him for a moment.

"I couldn't have taken it if you were sorry in any way that this happened."

She gave a soft chuckle. "There's no way I'm sorry. Not at all."

"Still, I owe you an apology."

"Why?" She blew a warm breath over his chest hairs and watched them move.

"Because I couldn't wait. Once we got in here, I lost it. I wanted you too much to take it slowly."

She chuckled again. "For future reference, I doubt very seriously if there is such a thing as you wanting me too much." She'd said *"future,"* she realized with a shock. For that moment, she'd allowed herself to think that the two of them could have a future. David had told her to try to believe it a day at a time. She was starting out with moments, but at least she was starting.

He stroked his hand up and down her arm. "I can't tell where the satin comforter ends and your skin begins."

"That's a very nice thing for you to say," she whispered.

" 'Nice' has nothing to do with it." He reached for her hand and entwined his fingers with hers. "It's the truth."

She moved, sliding her head off his chest to resettle in the crook of his arm, and angling her face up to him. She was rewarded when he bent his head and pressed a gentle kiss to her lips, then to her forehead.

If only she could freeze these precious moments, she reflected, these blissful moments spent lying in David's arms. If she could, then there would be no one trying to kill him, no more painful separations, no more arguments.

But she knew her wishes were futile. Tomorrow would come, and the danger would be there, and David would walk out the Tower's front door to put himself directly in the crosshairs of danger. And nothing she could do or say would change his mind.

All she could do was try to forget tomorrow and savor this time they had now. What had he said to her? *Live with him in the present.* It was going to take a lot of courage to do that, and she wasn't sure she was up to it. But for him she had to try.

"What are you thinking about?" he murmured, squeezing her hand.

"How happy I am at this moment." He kissed her forehead and she pulled her hand from his to let her fingers play over his body, exploring him, savoring the shape and textures of him. She traced a six-inch scar along his ribs. "I remember this. Libya, right?"

He chuckled. "Right. A knife fight that, appearances to the contrary, I won."

She pulled back from him so that she could see him better. "And here's that bullet wound from . . . was it also Libya?"

He grinned. "That's not a very lucky country for me."

"I guess it depends on your point of view. You're here now. I'd say you were pretty lucky to get out of there in one piece."

"Ummm, I guess you're right."

"I'm right about a lot of things," she said pointedly, then regretted it. Live in the present, she reminded herself. "I also seem to remember several scars on your back that you told me you received in Northern Africa *and* South America."

"You've got a good memory."

She smiled. "And obviously you have a lousy travel agency, since they constantly route you into war zones. If I were you, I'd have someone else make your travel arrangements from now on." She tried to keep her voice light, but then she saw something that pushed all else from her mind. "Wait. What's this?" She pointed to a red, angry scar an inch from his hipbone. As soon as she asked, she saw another wound above his waist, two or three inches in from his side. "And this? These are new, aren't they?"

His fingers slipped through her hair with an exquisitely delicate touch. "Yes."

"How new?"

"Three months ago."

"Three months ago? That's about the time you called me while I was en route to Allesandro's." She tried to sit up, but his arm around her tightened, keeping her by his side.

"It's nothing to get upset about," he murmured. "They're both healed.

"I won't get upset; just tell me what happened."

"It happened in the past, Kylie."

"Not that *far* in the past."

He sighed. "It happened during the first time we went in to get Asad. From the start, things didn't go right. For one thing, unanticipated help showed up for them. It was brutal and I wasn't the only one of our guys who was wounded. Scott and I called a retreat. We got out of there and the wounded were flown straight to Paris."

"So you were in the hospital when you called me?"

"No." He gently caressed her cheek. "I'd just gotten out and had checked into a hotel to finish recuperating."

"Why didn't you tell me you were injured?"

With a grin he looked down at her. "Why? What would you have done? Cancel your trip to Molinari's?"

"No."

"Would you have come to see me after the Molinari trip?"

"Probably not." She hated admitting that to him now, but it was the truth.

"Right," he said. "Then what purpose would it have served for you to know?"

"None, I suppose." Then she realized something that days ago would have shocked her, but now she accepted completely. If he'd told her he'd been wounded *and* had said that he needed her, she would have had the pilot head the plane straight for Paris. "How long did you allow yourself to heal? A couple of days?"

"Let's just say that when we went back in to get Asad the second time, I was fully healed." He reached for her and pulled her on top of him. "Now can we please get back to the present? It's *much* more interesting."

She smiled down at him. "In this particular instance, and *only* this one, you're right."

With a husky laugh, he rolled over on top of her.

◆────────◆

Kylie eased out from under David's arm and off the bed. For several moments she simply stood and watched him sleep. When he was awake, he looked tough, powerful, invincible. Incredibly, he looked the same even in sleep. But he wasn't invincible. The wounds on his body proved that he wasn't.

During the last few hours, they had made love to each other several more times. Hard, hot passion had blazed between them. There wasn't a place on her body he hadn't touched, kissed, or stroked. There wasn't a place on his body she hadn't explored with her mouth and hands.

At times their lovemaking had been so slow, sweet, and deeply emotional that as she'd climaxed, tears had run down her face. At other times their need for each other had accelerated so fast and had flamed so high, she'd barely been able to breathe. They'd been ravenous for each other with a need that at times had bordered on violence. Yet she didn't need to look in the mirror to know there wasn't a bruise on her.

She scooped up her gown and robe and quietly made her way out of her room to the bathroom of her guest bedroom. The last thing she wanted to do was awaken David by using the shower in her bathroom. When daylight came, he was going to need to be alert and on guard.

After she'd showered and slipped back into her gown and robe, she returned to the living room and settled into a comfortable chair. Their lovemaking had left her exhausted, but she couldn't allow herself to go to sleep. She needed to stay awake until David left.

"What's wrong, Kylie?"

Her head jerked around. David filled the hall doorway. A towel was wrapped around his hips and his hair was wet. He'd obviously taken a shower while she was taking hers. "Why are you awake?"

"You woke me when you got out of bed."

"I'm sorry. I was trying to let you sleep."

Studying her, he smiled slightly. "It wasn't your fault. Years in the field have taught me to be a very light sleeper."

"Why didn't you say something?"

"I didn't know you weren't coming right back. But after a few minutes when you didn't come back, I realized what you'd done."

"So you took a shower too." She shrugged. "I'd hoped you'd be able to get some sleep."

"Come back to bed and I will."

She shook her head. "I can't, but please, you go back. You're going to need all the sleep you can get for tomorrow."

"And you're not?" Suddenly he crouched in front of her, his powerful thighs supporting him and pushing against the towel, parting the edges halfway up. "What's wrong, Kylie?"

"Nothing."

"I don't believe you. There's something wrong, and if you don't tell me, I'll go get dressed, come back in here, and sit up with you. And then neither one of us will get any sleep." His tone had been gentle and patient, but there was no doubt in her mind that he was serious.

He started to rise, but she put her hand on his shoulder, still damp from his shower. "Can't you just go back to bed?"

"Only if you come with me."

She drew in a deep breath. "If I do, I might fall asleep, and I don't want to do that."

"Why?"

She looked at him. "Because I don't want to wake up in the morning and find you gone."

He stared at her for several moments, then slowly he shook his head. "It was that damned note, wasn't it? The note I left without waking you. Actually, it would probably be more accurate to say it's *still* the note, because plainly it still haunts you."

"It sounds silly, I know. I was twenty-one and I felt very adult, but in retrospect I guess I hadn't finished growing up."

"Honey, that wasn't immaturity. It was simply a reaction that came from your past. If you'd been fifty, your reaction could well have been the same and it would have been just as understandable."

"I don't know." She glanced down at her tightly entwined hands in her lap and couldn't remember twisting them together. "When I read your note—"

"You flashed back to the note your mother had left you."

She nodded. "But I didn't figure that out until much later. At first I was just hurt."

"And then you became angry." He gently pulled her hands apart so that he could hold one. "From some of the things you've said these last twenty-four hours, I was finally able to figure it all out." He squeezed her hand. "I'm so sorry, Kylie. At the time, it never occurred to me that my note would take you back to that early trauma."

"Of course it didn't. I didn't even realize it myself for quite some time. My reaction wasn't your fault, David. Or strictly speaking, even mine, I suppose. It was something beyond my control."

He looked down at her hand, then returned his gaze to her, his expression grim. "If anyone should have been able to put two and two together, it should have been me. I was there, damn it. I saw firsthand what you went through."

She shook her head. "There's no use playing the could've, would've, should've game. It's in the past now."

"You're right. The past is behind us, but if it still bothers you . . ." Holding her hand, he stood and drew her to her feet. "Does it?"

"The thought of waking up tomorrow and not finding you there beside me bothers me a lot."

"I'll be there," he said solemnly. "I promise you." He slid his arm around her. "Come on, sweetheart. We both need some sleep."

She edged out of his grasp so that she could look up into his eyes. "There's something else I need to tell you."

"Then tell me."

"First I want to apologize to you for my behavior these past years. It's been deplorable."

"It's past, remember?"

"A lot is past. A lot isn't. Just listen to me, David. Please."

"I'm listening. Whatever it is, together we can fix it."

He was so confident, so strong, and she was trying her best to emulate him, but with the approaching day her fears were creeping out.

"After figuring out the emotional impact the note had on me, I could have explained the matter to you and I knew you would have understood. But I also realized there was something else going on. I didn't want to open a dialogue with you about *anything*, because somewhere in the back of my mind I knew that if I spent more than a few minutes alone with you, we'd end up making love. And I knew . . ."

Her throat clogged, forcing her to stop. She could feel tears gathering in her eyes.

"What?" he asked softly. "You can tell me anything."

Determinedly she blinked the tears away, cleared her throat, and started again. "I couldn't risk falling in love with you again when I knew your next mission could mean that you'd come home in a body bag."

"I see." He stared at her thoughtfully. "And is that still how you feel?"

Yes, she wanted to scream, but she didn't. No matter what she was feeling, no matter what she said to him, he'd still walk out of the Tower tomorrow to face an enemy. He didn't need to take her baggage with him.

"Actually," she began slowly, "I've discovered tonight that it's useless to try to prevent myself from falling in love with you because I'm already in love with you. The truth is, I've loved you since I was five. I loved you the night of my twenty-first birthday party. I loved you during the seven years we were apart. I love you now. I will always love you." She stopped, allowing her breath to even out, and she discovered that David didn't even seem to be breathing at all. "As for the part about being so afraid that you'll be killed—let's just say I'm working very hard on it."

For several moments he was silent as varying expressions chased across his face. Finally he spoke. "My God, Kylie, what did I ever do to deserve you? Whether you know it or not, you are an extremely remarkable woman. You've had so much pain in your life, and I unknowingly added to it. But you've had the courage to face your fears and come out of it even stronger."

She tried to smile but failed. "I wouldn't be so sure about that last part. The outcome is still in doubt."

"No, it's not." He gently took her face in his hands. "Kylie, everything you said about loving me rings true for me too. I've loved you forever. The reason I've never been able to get you out of my mind is that you're so much a part of me." He grinned slightly. "You always have been, even when I didn't want you to be. But you're in my blood for good, and nothing and no one will ever get you out. I love you, Kylie, and please believe me when I say that we're going to have a wonderful life together."

Kylie awakened first. David still held her, his body spooned tightly around her, his arm over her waist. She couldn't have moved if she wanted to, which she didn't. It was already light outside and she knew that soon enough he'd wake and leave.

She lay quiet and tried to focus on what was happening right then, in the present. She wanted to fill up her senses with everything about the moment. She wasn't nearly as strong as David thought she was. She was scared to death of the future . . . the future that would start only a couple of hours from now.

So she set about trying to memorize the calm and serenity that she was feeling now, knowing that as long as he lay in her bed holding her, he was safe. She wanted to remember the strong, steady sound of his breathing and his unique, exotic scent. And she didn't ever want to forget the weight of his arm over her waist, as if even asleep his instinct was to keep her close to him.

But . . . She closed her eyes and a tear escaped to slide down her cheek. *She couldn't do it.* No matter how hard she tried, she couldn't get it out of her mind that, after today, all of the sensations she was trying so desperately to remember were sensations she might not ever be able to feel again.

David stirred. Instantly she tried to slow her breathing so that he would think she was still asleep, but she should have known she couldn't fool him.

His fingers brushed her hair off her face and away from her neck, then he leaned over and kissed the sensitive spot at the base of her ear.

"Good morning," he murmured, his voice warm and caressing. One more sound to try to remember.

Discreetly brushing away the tear, she rolled over

and smiled. "Good morning. Did you get as much sleep as you needed?"

"As much as I needed?" He grinned. "Probably not. But I got enough."

"Enough? You mean, enough being the hours we *weren't* making love?"

He chuckled. "I'd rather make love with you than sleep anytime, day or night."

Her smile slipped. "I wanted you to be rested today so that you'd be alert."

"I don't need much sleep to be alert."

There was no point in debating the point with him or even worrying about it. Last night, they'd each wanted each other too much to allow much time for rest. She ran her hand down the side of his face and felt the scratchiness of his overnight's growth of beard. Another texture to memorize. "Would you like to take a shower before you leave?"

"I probably should, but not with you." He grinned. "If I hauled you in there with me like I want to, I'd never leave."

She smiled at the playfulness in his voice. "Oh, I see. *I'm* too much of a temptation, which means it's all *my* fault for not letting you sleep last night or allowing you to get a decent shower this morning. I don't *think* so, David."

He laughed. "It's absolutely your fault."

"*Not*," she said and proceeded to attack him, pummeling him with powder-puff-soft hits until he cried out for mercy because he was laughing so hard.

Fifteen minutes later, she lay on the bed, propped

up against a pile of pillows, and watched as he dressed. While he'd showered, she'd gone across the hall to Wyatt's apartment and found a fresh set of clothes for him. "What about breakfast?"

"I'm having it with Scott. Remember?"

She hadn't. She'd only been thinking that if she could talk him into breakfast, she'd have him with her for that much longer. "How about taking Tim and a couple of guards with you?" He slanted her a look that had her sighing inwardly. She'd had to try.

Finished dressing, he sat down on the bed beside her and took her hand. "How about this? I'll try to check in with you every few hours."

"How? On a cell phone that can be traced?"

"Scott is bringing me a new state-of-the-art digital cell that is practically untraceable."

"Isn't that what you thought about your other?"

"No," he said gently. "Actually, I didn't even think. Remember? I let my guard down, which I won't do again. But to try to allay your fears, I'll call you from a pay phone, if I can find one."

"Perfect. Then you'll be standing still."

He chuckled. "You are a *hard* woman to please."

She was trying to keep things light, but as the time went by, it was getting harder for her. "Damn you, David. You're acting like you're just going out for the morning paper. The truth is, I should bash you over the head with a blunt object, then tie you up and keep you here."

"Tie me up and keep me here?" His eyes glinting, he reached over and tucked a strand of her hair behind her ear. "I didn't know you were into kinky, but hey, babe, as soon as I get back, I'm your guy."

She could feel herself about to burst into tears, so she balled her fist and hit him in the shoulder. As far as she could tell, he didn't even feel her punch, which made her angrier.

He went to rise, but she grabbed his arm and pulled him back down by her side. "You listen to me, David Galado. Tomorrow night is Abigail's Christmas Eve party and you've got another thing coming if you think I'm going without a date."

"I must have forgotten," he said, humor glittering in his eyes. "Did I invite you?"

"No, *I* invited *you*. Just a moment ago. Didn't you hear me? David, I'm *serious*. You've got to be there." The party wasn't what was important. That he return to her alive was.

His humor vanished. "Now you listen to me," he said, taking both her hands in his and gazing deeply into her eyes. "Nothing is going to happen to me, Kylie. *Nothing*. Trust me on that. But as for Abigail's party, I can't promise you anything. I don't know how long it's going to take us to get Hassan. But what I *can* say is that if it is at all possible, I will be there. Maybe not in time for the first dance, but in plenty of time for the last."

Her bottom lip trembled traitorously. "You'll really try?"

"Absolutely. And do you know why?"

"Because I'll kill you if you don't?"

"No. Because I love you and wherever you are is

where I want to be. And now that I know you love me, you've given me an even greater reason to make it back to you as soon as possible."

"I love you," she whispered and lifted her face for a final kiss.

TEN

Kylie's private line rang around eleven that morning and she immediately grabbed the receiver. "Yes?"

"Did I catch you at a busy time?"

The sound of David's voice made her weak with relief. "Oh, right, like I'd be too busy to talk to you this morning. Are you okay?"

He chuckled. "Yes."

She heard noise in the background—traffic, horns, a screech of tires, a drone of indistinguishable voices. He was out in the open. "Is your friend with you?"

"Scott?" His voice faded as if he had turned his head away from the phone, then his voice returned. "He's around here somewhere."

The man who was supposed to be guarding David's back was around there *somewhere*? She swallowed, determined to keep her jittery nerves to herself. She'd already said her piece. "Have you made any progress?"

"It's still early to say anything for sure."

"Then just tell me you've got people who are watching out for you. Specifically, men with guns. *Big* guns."

"I've got all the protection I need. Didn't I tell you that everything's going to go fine?"

She closed her eyes. "That's what you told me."

"So just keep remembering that and stop worrying." Urgency suddenly infused his tone. "I've got to go. I love you and I'll try to call back, but if you don't hear from me, don't worry. It just means I'm getting closer."

"Wait, David. Don't hang—" The line went dead.

She slammed the phone on its cradle and tossed her pen down on her desk. "Yeah, right, David," she muttered. "Don't worry. Everything's going to be fine." She rubbed her forehead. 'So then why do I have this really awful feeling that it's not?"

The next few hours passed slowly. Thankfully she had work on which she could focus. But it was hard. She jumped every time Clifford buzzed her intercom to announce a call. Her heart skipped a beat every time her door opened. But her private line didn't ring again. And as the hours ticked by and there was no more word from David, her nerves wound tighter and tighter.

The intercom buzzed again. "Yes?"

"Ms. Damaron, there's a Mr.—"

Her door opened and a tall, blond-haired man with steel blue eyes walked in.

"Scott Hewitt," he said, crossing the carpet to her desk.

Clifford rushed in behind him. "I'm sorry, Ms.

Damaron. I tried to explain to this gentleman that you were not seeing anyone today, but—"

She stood, her gaze locked with Scott's. "It's David, isn't it? Something's happened to him."

Scott nodded.

"Ms. Damaron, would you like me to call security?"

With a flick of her wrist, she waved Clifford out of the room. "Is David dead?"

He hesitated. "Not to my knowledge."

"Not to your *knowledge?*"

"I'm sorry. We really don't know much at this point. But David made me promise to come and tell you in person if anything happened to him. I probably should have waited until we knew something more, but the next hours are going to be very busy for us."

She wrapped her arms around her waist and held herself rigid. "Tell me exactly what happened."

"As I said, I can't tell you much. We had David covered. One moment he was there, the next he wasn't."

"You're telling me no one saw him *disappear?*"

"Yes and no."

Her anger flared to life. "What in the hell does that mean?"

"No one actually saw him grabbed," he said calmly, "but we did see a black van drive away from the spot where he'd been. We had three cars standing by to tail them, but we lost the van in traffic. We got the license number, though, which is being checked out as we speak."

This was a nightmare, Kylie thought. A full-blown

nightmare. "And what if they had the forethought to steal that license plate before they put it on the van?"

"Then we'll find some other way." He glanced at his watch. "Now if you'll excuse me—"

"Not yet." She had started to shake, but she managed to point a finger at him. "You had one job and that was to keep David alive, and you seriously bungled it. So you can wait one more minute and tell me the truth. Do you think David is dead?"

This time he didn't hesitate. "No. We're banking on Hassan keeping him alive, at least through tonight and maybe tomorrow." He paused. "Kylie, it was a part of our plan to have David kidnapped."

"Part of your *plan?*" In disbelief, she hit her forehead with the heel of her palm. "For God's sake, a baboon could have come up with a better plan than that one." But even as she said it, she knew who had come up with the plan. It had been David.

"It was the fastest way we could think of to get to Hassan," Scott continued steadily. "Our plan was for Hassan to grab David and for us to follow. If we lost them, we'd go electronic and follow the tracking device we put on David."

"Tracking device?" she asked, new hope entering her voice.

He shook his head. "They found the tracking device right away, along with the wire he was wearing. We also had several other backup plans, but Hassan and his men are slick."

"I thought your organization was elite. The best of the best. What's wrong with you all? You lost *David.* How could you have allowed that to happen?" Somewhere in the back of her mind, she knew Scott wasn't to blame, but right at that moment, anger was the only weapon she had to keep her from completely falling apart.

"New York City is not our jungle, Kylie, but unfortunately, it's Hassan's and his men's. Even so, they're still not as good as we are. All we need to do is find out where they are and then we're in and we'll get David."

"How can you be so sure you'll find David alive? He's Hassan's number one target."

"Exactly. But Hassan is also practical. First, they're going to try to get information out of him about our organization. They'll want names and locations of our agents, the depth of our information we have on them and others, and any and all plans we have for the future."

"David won't tell them anything."

For the first time she saw Scott's gaze briefly soften on her. "I know, but it will take time for them to realize it. And during that time, they'll be . . . trying to break David. Then once they realize he won't talk, they'll start killing him. Slowly. Hassan hates David so much that he'll want him to suffer as much as possible before he kills him."

Her face paled. "They'll torture him."

Scott nodded. "As awful as that fact is, it will buy us some much-needed time. Every minute counts, which is exactly why I need to leave now."

"Wait."

"Kylie—"

She held out her hand. "I know. Believe me, I understand that I'm asking for precious minutes that involve David's life." Her voice broke, but she went on. "Please, just tell me what you'll be looking for." Her voice was regaining its firmness, her trembling slowly easing. Scott's use of the word *jungle* had triggered an idea.

"An address. A location. We're feeding the computer every name we have on them, in every kind of combination we can think of, hoping we'll come up with an address we haven't yet found and searched."

"Are you looking for a particular kind of address, such as a house or an apartment?"

He hesitated, his gaze assessing her, but then he went on, talking fast. "The place we're looking for, they've had for a while. It's got to have the space that would hold not only Hassan and his group, but their stockpile of weapons and bomb-making materials, plus whatever they are using for a cover."

"Cover? You mean, for instance, if they told everyone they sold priceless vases from the Middle East, they'd need to have enough vases to make a convincing show?"

"That's right. Whatever they're using for their cover, the items and the crates that the product is being shipped in have to be big enough to hide their shipments of weapons parts."

She nodded, her mind assimilating the information as rapidly as it was coming at her. "I understand. Thank you for explaining." Now that she had a clear picture of what the situation was, she no longer felt helpless, because she knew there was something she could do. "Probably a warehouse, right?"

"Right," Scott said, his face grim. "Unfortunately,

the number of warehouses in the area is astronomical.
But we've got to start somewhere and we're going to
focus our attentions on the harbor, specifically the in-
dustrial docks along the waterfront where they off-load
goods. But again, this state has a long shoreline."

"Do you have any pictures or drawings of Hassan
and his men?"

Impatience was beginning to creep into Scott's expression. He glanced pointedly at his watch. "Yes.
We've managed to get the college graduation pictures
of Hassan and a few of his buddies."

"How soon can you get them faxed to me?" He
started to shake his head, but Kylie cut him off. "Don't
bother to tell me that it's classified information. You
need all the help you can get, and I'm in a position to
do just that."

Scott studied her, seeming to weigh his choices.
"How?"

"How is not important but I'll make you a deal.
Give me a secure number where I can reach you, and if
I'm able to find out any information, I'll let you know
immediately."

He shook his head.

"Look, I'm offering you help—help that you're in
no position to turn down if you want to get David out
alive."

Scott considered her for a moment, then blew out a
long breath. "Okay. I can have the pictures faxed to
you."

She grabbed a pen and scrawled across a white
notepad. "This is my fax number," she said. "This second one is a number I will answer anytime, night or

day. Please call if you hear anything, *anything* at all, and I'll do the same for you." She ripped off the note sheet and handed it to him, then took from him the number he'd written on the back of a card. "Thank you."

He pocketed the note and was nearly to the door when he stopped and looked back at her. "David was right—you're really something. You should receive the faxes within the next five minutes. Oh, and Kylie? One more thing. If you pray, now would be a great time. We're going to have to be very lucky to get to David before—" He broke the sentence off. "Just pray."

With the faxes from Scott on her desk, she looked up the number in her private book of phone numbers and dialed.

"Hello."

"Allesandro, I'm so glad you're there."

"Kylie? Is anything wrong?"

"Something is very wrong, but don't worry. What I told you last night still holds. I'm not the one in danger, but David is."

"David? Your driver?"

"David is not a driver for our family, Allesandro. To make a long story short, he's an old family friend who works for the government and he's been kidnapped by terrorists here in the city, which is why I need your immediate help."

"Terrorists . . . ? I would do anything for you, Kylie, you know that. But in this case, I don't understand how I can help. The FBI could probably give you more help than I can, or perhaps some other government organization."

"Not for what I have in mind. Just listen. New York is your jungle, Allesandro—your backyard. You know just about everything that happens here. As soon as we finish talking, I want to fax you the pictures of four of the men who've kidnapped David, and I'd like you to fax the pictures to as many of your people as you can and as soon as possible. My hope is that someone will recognize one or more of these terrorists and call you with their location. Tell them warehouses are a good bet, perhaps along the waterfront."

"You have an excellent mind, Kylie. Your plan sounds infinitely doable. Fax me the pictures."

"Thank you, Allesandro. I knew I could count on you. Oh, one more thing. Make sure your people know they're not to take any action other than to call you with the location. Then you call me and I'll contact David's organization. They'll take it from there. None of your people will be involved."

"All right. Anything else?"

"Just that time is critical. The longer they have David . . . Just tell everyone to work fast."

"I will." He paused. "Kylie?"

"Yes?"

"Two nights ago I asked you if there was someone else. You said there was someone, but that he was too difficult to love. The man to whom you were referring was this David, wasn't he?"

"Yes."

"And you love him despite the fact that he's difficult."

"Yes, I do."

He was silent for several moments. "Go ahead and get the pictures to me, and I'll get back to you as soon as I find out anything."

"Thank you, Allesandro. I'm very grateful."

Kylie told Clifford to go home, then called Jonah, Sin, Lion, and Yasmine into her office and filled them in on everything she knew. They immediately began to toss around ideas, trying to come up with something they could do to help. In the end, though, they had to admit that all they could do was wait. Unfortunately, none of them was good at waiting.

When her private line rang, they all jumped.

Kylie snatched up the phone. "Yes?"

"I've come up with an address," Allesandro said.

Tears of relief sprang into her eyes. "Thank heavens."

She proceeded to copy down not only the address, but tactical details about the building. And as she took down the information, another idea began to form in her head.

"My cousin, Gilberto, is the one who gave me all of this," Allesandro said. "He's in a high position in the union down on the docks. Use him as your contact. He'll be waiting for your call and he's eager to help. He says these men you're looking for aren't particularly well liked down there."

He reeled off a number and she wrote it down. "Allesandro, I can't thank you enough."

She hung up and swept a gaze over her cousins.

"There's no hard evidence that David is at this address Allesandro just gave me, but the men who were in the pictures leased this warehouse three years ago." She lifted the receiver and dialed. Scott answered immediately. "How far away are you from the Tower?" she asked.

"Ten minutes at the most. Why?"

"I've just been given an address and the setup of a warehouse down at the harbor, along with the name and number of a contact who identified the men in the pictures you faxed me. He said they've been leasing the warehouse for the last three years. This same contact is also standing by in case we need him."

"Wait. Back up. How did you get this information?"

"I can't tell you his name, but I trust him implicitly."

"So you're asking me to commit my men to a mission on the basis of an unidentified source?"

"He's not unidentified to me. I'd trust him with my life. And you will be able to talk with the contact who identified the pictures. Besides, have you been able to uncover anything?"

"Not yet."

"Look. Don't turn this down until you see this information. Can you come here, or shall I come where you are?"

"Tell me over the phone," Scott answered quickly.

"No. I don't mean to be difficult, and I'm fully aware of the importance of acting as fast as possible, but I truly believe the odds of getting David out of there alive will increase if I'm there."

"If you're there? There's no way in hell I can let you go, Kylie. My organization uses civilians only for information. We never involve them in our operations. More importantly, David would kill me if something happened to you."

"Scott, there's too little time for us to argue about this. I've got the address, and what's more, I have the means to tackle this alone if necessary." She was bluffing. The Damaron guards were capable of doing what it would take to free David, but it would take time to assemble and brief them and then decide on a strategy.

"You'll do that only if you want David dead. Kylie, my men and I are standing by, ready to go. All we need is the information you have. We could have David home in a couple of hours."

"I'll make you another deal, Scott." She heard him groan, but she ignored the sound. "As soon as I see you, I'll tell you everything I know and lay out my plan. If you still don't think it's a good idea, after you've heard me out, and you can convince me why it's not, I'll stay home. Now, do you want to come here? If so, you can use our private parking level as a staging area for your men. Or I can come there, but it's going to take me about twenty minutes. Tell me which you'd prefer."

He exhaled loudly. "It's better if you come here."

"I'll be there as fast as I can." After receiving directions to Scott's location, she hung up the phone, then hurried toward the door. "Call Tim and tell him to have my Jag ready in ten minutes."

Her cousins surged to their feet. Joshua reached inside his jacket pocket for his cell phone.

"Wait, Kylie." Sin grabbed her arm just outside her office. "What are you going to do?"

"Come with me to my apartment and I'll tell you all everything. Yasmine, you can help me change clothes."

Kylie followed Scott's directions as she took another turn, heading toward the harbor area. She was thankful that once she'd laid out Allesandro's information and her idea to Scott, he'd bought it.

She wasn't kidding herself. Scott and his team didn't need her participation. In truth, her part would be very small. But she hadn't been able to stand the thought of sitting back at the Tower doing nothing but waiting, and she sensed that Scott had finally been won over by the knowledge that she was the one person in the world who wanted David back more than he did. So he'd relented, but only after extracting a promise that she would do exactly as he said.

Her cousins hadn't acquiesced quite as easily to her plan. They'd argued with her the whole time she was getting ready to go. At one point, they'd insisted, they should follow her at a distance. But in the end they'd given in to her, because they loved her enough to honor her wishes.

She'd been full of bravery with them and then with Scott, but now she was trembling and her stomach was knotted with nerves. But the image of David hurt, and maybe dying, kept her going forward.

She threaded her Jaguar through side streets and alleys, drawing closer to her destination. Because it was

Christmas Eve, the area was nearly deserted. She'd learned Hassan's warehouse was not directly on the water, but already there was a faint smell of brine in the air. Then she saw it, the warehouse where she prayed they'd find David, alive and well.

She turned off the headlights and the engine and allowed the car to roll to a stop fifteen yards short of the warehouse. She couldn't see Scott or any of his men, though she knew they wouldn't be doing their job if she could. Allesandro's cousin was also around somewhere. He'd already talked with Scott and helped him out with extra details about the place.

The warehouse looked dark except for a single light burning above the small stoop. The sign over the doorway proclaimed, PERSIAN IMPORTS. Gilberto had told them this entrance was the one they used as their front door. He'd also told Scott to expect the warehouse to look dark from the outside, since they'd painted the high windows black and had added blackout shades.

She glanced at her watch to assure herself she was still on schedule, then pushed the button to pop the car's hood. Her key ring held an ornamental charm that in truth was a small canister of pepper spray. It would be good for only a few shots and was her only weapon. Taking her keys with her, she slid out of the car and quietly closed its door. Immediately she felt a cold wind whip around the buildings to slap against her bare skin.

She was wearing a short slip of a dress, cut on the bias out of sterling-silver-colored satin jersey. The dress clung to her every curve in an exquisitely unforgiving manner that made any type of underwear impossible, and appeared a mere breath away from falling off her. An extravagant circle of diamonds sparkled at her neck and wrist, and more diamonds dripped from her ears.

She raised the hood of her car, checked her watch one more time, then, in her four-inch silver heels, she walked to the door. Listening for a moment, she didn't hear anything. She was still trembling, but now it was not only from fear, but from the cold, which she hoped would play in her favor.

Staring at the door, she deliberately thought of the saddest, most devastating thing she could imagine. There was no contest. The idea of being too late and finding David already dead was almost too painful for her to bear. As she'd hoped, tears began to roll down her cheeks. Then and only then did she raise her hand to the door and knock. When after several moments she didn't hear anything, she knocked louder.

ELEVEN

An impatient voice yelled back at her, "We're closed!"

Shivering, she pounded on the door. "Please open the door. My car has broken down and there's no one around to help me. *Please*."

Suddenly the door opened and a man stuck his head out. "Go away. We're closed."

She slid one silver-clad foot across the threshold and leaned sideways so that she could better see the man's face, and more importantly, so that he could see her. One thing she knew. This man wasn't one of the four that Scott had faxed her.

"I *can't* go anywhere," she said plaintively, tears streaming down her face. "It's my car. It just stopped and I don't have a clue why." She pointed toward the red Jaguar and had the satisfaction of having him open the door a little wider so that he could see where she pointed. "I was invited to a party and I was positive it was somewhere around here." She paused to wipe the tears from her face. "But now I'm not so sure. I've been driving around for hours."

She edged closer to him so that the light above the door now shone directly down on her, along with a beam of inside light. When he looked back at her, she saw his eyes widen when he finally noticed the half a million dollars' worth of diamonds, along with the dress she was almost wearing.

"I'm afraid I'm hopelessly lost." She smiled up at him through her tears. "Please tell me you can help me."

She heard a couple of more gruff voices asking what the problem was, then two more faces appeared in the doorway, causing the door to open wider. This time she was able to step over the threshold and into the warehouse. However, as badly as she wanted to look around for David, she kept her wide, teary eyes focused on the three men who were now actively studying every inch of her.

"Please don't turn me away," she begged, looking at each man in turn, even though their gazes had turned greedy and predatory as they eyed the diamonds and the perilously low neckline of her dress. She wrapped her arms around herself so that her breasts mounded uncertainly above the dress. "Please. I'm cold. Could I come in? I need to use your phone."

Another voice sounded behind the three men—a hard, cutting voice that made the men jump. Then a face appeared to match the voice. He was one of the men whose picture she'd seen.

She focused on him. "I've been trying to explain to these nice men that my car has broken down and I really need to use your phone." She dropped her voice as if she were imparting confidential information. "I'm afraid I'm terribly late for a party."

He simply stared at her and she knew what he was seeing. Because of the cold and her fear, her rigid nipples were straining against the satin jersey. Goose bumps decorated the tops of her breasts and along her arms. Then there were the diamonds that sparkled and dazzled with the promise of money.

The men outrightly ogled her, which was exactly what she hoped they'd do, even if in some way she was setting back the women's movement twenty years.

She looked back at the fourth man. "Please, if you would just let me come in and call my mechanic, I would be forever in your debt."

"No, no, no," he finally said, though his eyes were locked on her breasts and the diamonds. "I'm sorry, but you must go."

Shouting in a foreign language, another man came running up to those who were standing in a semicircle around her. The men near her stiffened at whatever he was saying, but none of them moved away. The new man had to push through them to get to her. She decided not to give him any time to react to her.

Dredging up more tears, she grabbed the lapels of his jacket and immediately launched into her story. "You *must* help me. I was trying to find a party, but I got lost. . . . You don't happen to know of a party going on down here, do you?

None of them answered. If any had weapons, she couldn't see them. Between their shoulders, she could see another man rapidly approaching. That meant she had managed to pull six men away from what they had been doing, and, she hoped, their weapons.

She directed her tear-drenched blue eyes to the sixth man. "Please tell me you have a pot of hot tea brewing. That would be just heaven—"

Thunder rolled through the building. The sixth man turned and uttered what had to be a profanity.

A shout came from the other end of the warehouse. All six men spun toward the sounds and saw the heavy metal dock doors roll ponderously up. Several men who had been sitting around a table scrambled to their feet and rushed toward the opening doors, but they ran headlong into a team of Scott's men.

At the same time, explosions detonated and chain-locked doors located around the warehouse burst open, and more of Scott's men swarmed in. Shots were fired, then automatic gunfire erupted.

Three of the men with her whipped their arms around behind them and pulled handguns from their belts. The sixth man yelled something at their group and five of them took off, but they were obviously caught off guard, giving Scott's team an obvious edge. She prayed it would be enough. The man who had been left with her gazed worriedly after them.

Grabbing the few seconds he unwittingly was giving her, she jabbed one four-inch heel down on his instep. He yelped and instinctively bent forward toward his foot, but she stopped him, thrusting the heel of her hand upward to his nose. Cartilage crunched and he cried out in pain. She finished him off with a blast of pepper spray, then whirled around and allowed herself to take in the scene in the warehouse.

Confusion reigned. Shouts echoed off the high ceiling. Shots reverberated down the long warehouse. Men were everywhere. She recognized Scott's men because they were dressed in black, but in the melee she couldn't tell how many of Hassan's men there were.

Crates were piled high in neat rows toward the back. She saw a forklift, pallet jacks, several dollies, and large hanging lights. Another area had been closed off to use as an office. She hoped that was where they were keeping David.

Scott had told her that as soon as she saw his men enter the warehouse she should run to her car and drive home. Normally she obeyed orders that involved her security, but this time she couldn't. It would take an act of God to make her leave before she knew if David was there and if he was alive or dead.

She glanced down at the man writhing in pain on the floor, clawing at his face. He'd be all right by the time Scott and his men were ready to take him and his cohorts into custody. In the meantime, he was currently in no position to hurt anyone else.

Kicking off her high heels and stooping low, she dashed along the wall, using boxes and crates to hide her progress.

She made it to the office and reached for the doorknob. It wouldn't turn. Her heart was hammering so loudly she could barely hear the gunfire anymore. Perspiration broke out on her forehead as she tried again. A shot struck the doorjamb above her head. This time the knob turned, just as another shot hit somewhere nearby. She dove into the room, hurriedly pushed herself to her feet, and flung her body against the door to shut it.

David.

He sat motionless, his hands and feet tied to a chair, his back to the door, his head down. Please let him be alive, she prayed.

She circled the chair and knelt in front of him. His face was bruised and, in places, swollen. A cut slashed his jaw. Blood crusted on his forehead. More blood rivered from a corner of his mouth. A gag was stuffed in his mouth and tied there by a length of black material knotted at the back of his head.

But thank God he was breathing.

Her hands shook as she reached up and gently untied the knot and removed the gag. "David?"

His eyes flew open. "Kylie? What in the *hell* are you doing here?"

Her hand flew to her heart. "Good God, David! Thank heavens! I thought you were unconscious." Tears of joy flooded her eyes. If he was strong enough to yell at her, he was going to be all right.

One of his eyes was partially swollen, but that didn't stop him from scouring her with an angry golden gaze that raked her up and down. "I wasn't. Now tell me why in hell you did such a stupid thing, coming here. And by the way, *why* are you dressed like a hooker?"

His anger took her aback. She stood and pressed a hard kiss to the portion of his mouth that wasn't bleeding, then shoved the gag back in his mouth. "I'm here because I'm saving your life, you ungrateful jerk. It's also the reason I'm dressed this way, thank you very much."

She went around him to untie the rope that bound his wrists, but David spit the gag out and pulled his wrists and legs apart. The ropes fell to the floor.

Scott burst through the door, his automatic weapon at the ready. When he saw the two of them, he relaxed. "Hassan and his crew are in cuffs. Two casualties and one injured on their side. No one seriously hurt on our side. How are you, David?"

David stood and shot a grim look at Scott over his shoulder. "Fine."

"Yeah, you look it," he said with a grin, surveying his friend's bruised and swollen face.

"He'd already managed to untie himself," Kylie told Scott. "He was pretending to be unconscious, probably in the hopes that he could catch one or two of them off guard and escape, but it never would have worked. Then I guess when he heard the shots he decided it would be best to play dead until he found out who was doing the shooting."

Scott chuckled. "Excellent assessment. Anytime you want a job with us, just let me know."

David kicked his feet free of the ropes and turned toward them. "You want to tell me why Kylie's here, Scott?"

"Good question. Kylie?" he said calmly. "I thought I told you to head for home once the shooting started. By the way, you did a brilliant job on those guys. From what I could tell, you had them completely unstrung. They were so busy looking at you, they wouldn't have known which way was up if you had pointed."

She smiled at him. "Thanks."

"What guys?" David barked to Scott, then turned to her. "And what did you do to them?"

With an overly sweet smile, Kylie stooped to retrieve the gag. "Since you were the one who said I was dressed like a hooker, you can probably figure it out for yourself. Scott, I assume you're going to need David to be debriefed and to be checked out by a doctor."

"That's right."

"Then I'll make you a deal." Scott gave an exaggerated groan and she laughed. "I'll leave him with you, but I'm giving you the responsibility of getting him to Abigail's party in"—she glanced at her watch—"three hours."

"Three hours will be cutting it close, Kylie."

"Then skip the debriefing and just get him to a doctor. Or do both at the same time. You work it out." She paused, thinking. "I guess I'll accept three and a half hours if I have to, but no more. And whatever you do, get some ice for his face as soon as possible. We don't want to scare the party guests, not to mention Abigail."

"I happen to be right here," David said, his voice dangerously soft. "Talk to *me*."

"I will." With a tender kiss to his cheek, she stuffed the gag back in his mouth. "Tonight. See you there too, Scott. 'Bye."

The drapes were pulled back in Abigail's huge drawing room so that everyone could see the falling snow. The delicate flakes coated the countryside and iced the peaks and valleys of Abigail's roof as if it were a cake. Adding to the delicate beauty of the fairyland ambience, tall firs, chestnuts, and maples twinkled with white lights.

Inside, a twenty-two-foot Christmas tree soared almost to the ceiling, decorated with colorful lights and family ornaments. Beneath it, gaily wrapped packages were piled high and deep, waiting to be opened tomorrow afternoon.

Large velvet red bows were spaced along the garlands of holly and fir that draped the mantel and stairway. Gold and red flames danced atop tall white and red candles.

On a small upstairs balcony that overlooked the room, a string quartet and a harpist were playing Christmas carols. The notes drifted down to the guests and floated in the air around them.

Absently fingering the sapphire heart she wore on a delicate gold chain, Kylie wound her way through the glittering crowd, stopping here and there to chat with old friends. She'd always loved Abigail's Christmas Eve parties. It was the perfect blend of family, old friends, and new.

"Kylie?"

Recognizing the voice, she whirled around. "Jo! Oh, I'm so glad you're finally here." She hugged her sister, then pulled back to look at her. Joanna's blond hair was drawn up into a sophisticated French twist and her elegant white silk gown accentuated her beauty. "I can't tell you how wonderful it is to see you."

Jo smiled. "You too, sweetheart. You'll never know how many times I thought of calling for a helicopter to take me into town so that I could see for myself how you were doing."

"You did the right thing by staying home. Your babies needed you. And as it turned out, I'm just fine."

"Well, I have to say you look more than just fine. You look absolutely glorious."

"Why, thank you," Kylie said, playfully turning as if she were modeling the blue velvet strapless gown. "I'm lucky enough to have a sister who's an incredibly talented designer, and this is just a little frock she whipped up for me in between changing diapers."

Jo laughed. "That diaper part is at least true, and so is the fact that you make a great walking advertisement for me. But it's not the dress that looks glorious. It's *you*. You're glowing. And speaking of which, when is—"

"Hi, you two," Yasmine said, joining them, wearing a black gown that glimmered with black cut-glass beads around its collar and cuffs. The effect made her amber eyes, hair, and skin look even more golden and radiant than they normally did. Truthfully, Yasmine could look radiant in a potato sack, but now she had an extra reason, the secret that Yasmine and Rio would tell everyone tomorrow afternoon. Next year at this time, they'd all have another baby to coo over.

"Kylie?"

She snapped out of her reverie and realized Yasmine had said something. "I'm sorry, Yaz. Did you ask me something?"

"I asked when you expected David."

"He should be here soon."

As she'd driven home from the warehouse, Kylie

had contacted her cousins back at the Tower to let them know everything had gone well. In their family, contacting one cousin meant contacting all her cousins, no matter where they were. Consequently, they all not only knew that she'd rushed out to try to help David, they also now knew the outcome.

She looked at Jo and Yasmine and suddenly something dawned on her. Her actions in rushing to David's aid had demonstrated better than any words how she felt about him. Then she realized something else.

She fixed Jo and Yasmine with a wry smile. "You've known all along that I was in love with David, haven't you? Everyone has known."

Yasmine smiled. "Oh, honey, we only had to see you look at him to know."

Jo nodded. "Even during the past several years when you avoided him and barely spoke to him. It was such a radical change from the way you'd always behaved around him that it was obvious there was something going on between you."

Kylie shook her head ruefully. "Glad to know I'm so transparent."

"Only when it comes to David, honey," said Yasmine.

"But why didn't any of you say anything to me about it?"

"Actually, I tried a couple of times," Jo said, "but you cut me off. In fact, whenever the subject of David came up, you'd usually leave the room. So we all decided it would be best to take a watch-and-wait attitude and to just be there for you in case you needed us."

Kylie shook her head in amazement. "How could I not have noticed that you all knew?"

Yasmine gave her a quick hug. "You were putting all your efforts into trying *not* to see anything that concerned David."

Full of emotion, she nodded. "I suppose you're right."

She was ecstatic that David was now safe. And yes, it was true that she loved David with all her heart and that he loved her. But she was smart enough to know their love didn't give them an automatic ticket for happiness that would last for the rest of their lives.

Just a few hours ago she'd been incredibly frightened for David. That particular danger had passed now, yet she knew tomorrow would bring new dangers for David, new challenges. It would also bring new challenges for her. She had no idea if she would be able to remain serene when the time came to see him off on his next mission. Nor did she know if she could be happy while she waited at home for months on end, never certain what he was doing or if he was even alive.

Soon, very soon, she'd have to make a decision about them. But not tonight. Tonight she and David deserved a time of undiluted joy and she could barely wait until he arrived.

Gabi strolled up, looking incredibly lovely, wearing an exquisite brown taffeta gown and a beautiful topaz teardrop necklace and earring set that Lion had given her on their wedding day. Gabi exchanged warm hellos with her sisters-in-law, then turned her gaze to Kylie. "I saw your necklace from across the room and just had to come over and see it up close. May I?"

"Of course."

Gabi slid her fingers beneath the heart-shaped sapphire and eyed it closer. "It's magnificent. Is it new?"

Jo arched an eyebrow at her sister. "That was going to be my next question to you."

Kylie grinned. "No, it's not new. I received it as a present on my twenty-first birthday."

Yasmine's mouth dropped. "From whom? And if you've had it all these years, why haven't we seen it before?"

Kylie looked over at Jo, who smiled back at her. "It was a gift from David, wasn't it?" Jo said.

Kylie nodded. "Yes, but it's been in my safe for the last seven years."

Gabi frowned. "Why—"

"Oh, girls there you are," Abigail said, rushing up to them in a swirl of red chiffon, a blaze of flaming red hair, and splashes of fire-engine-red nails and toenails. Oblivious to the fact that she was interrupting Gabi, she got right to the point. "Why aren't you girls circulating? Look over there at Lion and Sin. The two of them have been over there in that corner for the last ten minutes doing nothing but talking to each other."

She pointed her cigarette holder in the vague direction of the corner she meant. "Oh, and I see that Wyatt has joined them now. What am I going to do with you all?" She gave Gabi a plaintive look. "From the time they were born, this generation of Damarons has always preferred each other's company to that of anyone else's."

Gabi turned to Abigail. "In their defense, I would just like to point out that we've been standing here for several minutes and no one, absolutely *no one* has come up and tried to talk to us."

"Of course they haven't," Abigail said, her voice soothing, since Gabi was a relatively new member of the family. "One of you is enough to scare most anyone, darling, but two or more of you together is positively intimidating."

"Really? I guess I hadn't realized that. I don't remember being intimidated by Lion."

Even Abigail had to join Kylie, Yasmine, and Jo in laughing.

"I think *you* intimidated *him*," Yasmine said, still chuckling. "Or at the very least, seriously confused him."

Gabi gave a rueful grin. "Yeah, I guess you're right. When my grandmother told me he was one of *the* Damarons, I'm afraid my reaction was somewhat different than what Lion was accustomed to."

"I think you can safely say that," Yasmine said dryly.

Gabi turned back to Abigail. "Okay, this is what I'll do. I'll go get Lion and we promise to circulate."

"What a darling girl," Abigail said, pulling Gabi into a hug. When she'd finished, she sternly eyed her three great-nieces. "Now, girls. I expect you to do the same."

"Yes, ma'am," they all three said in unison.

"Oh, one more thing, Kylie," Abigail said. "Where is David?"

Kylie smiled. "He'll be here soon."

TWELVE

A warmth shivered down Kylie's spine. She turned and David was there, standing at the top of the steps that led down into the room, his gaze on her. In that moment, the room and the people disappeared and there was only him.

The swelling on his face looked better. A couple of the bruises looked worse. A bandage covered his lower right jaw, another curved over his left brow. No doubt those two wounds had required stitches. The right side of his lips was slightly swollen, and she could only imagine how sore and hurt the rest of his body was.

But as he came down the stairs and made his way toward her, he still moved with the animallike grace that was so uniquely his. Dressed in black tie and a tuxedo with a white shirt and a black tie, no swelling or bruising could detract from his force and magnetism. He was still the elegant savage she'd always known and always loved.

David worked his way through the crowd toward Kylie. If anyone spoke to him, he didn't hear them. If anyone was in his way, he didn't see them. Kylie was like his own personal lodestone. Everything in his body was urging him to get to her. Then finally he reached her, and for a moment all he could do was stare at her, trying to absorb every small detail about her.

He'd never seen her look more beautiful, more luminescent. Her blue eyes held such a loving expression as she gazed up at him that he could barely breathe. Her ivory skin gleamed, her blue velvet gown beguiled. But most of all, the sight of the sapphire heart that rested in the cleft of her breasts touched him to his very core.

Kylie was small, but she was the strongest, most powerful person he'd ever known, for she held his heart. Always had.

She lifted her hand to his face and gently touched a bruise. "I bet you're going to tell me that this looks worse than it feels."

He slowly smiled. "Actually it hurts much worse than it looks."

She chuckled. "You deserve it for not listening when I told you to stay with me so that you'd be safe."

He lifted the sapphire and fingered it. "Believe me, you got your retribution and more when you talked Scott into letting you take part in the rescue. My heart nearly stopped when I heard you call my name."

"You think I felt great when I saw you bound and gagged, with blood caked on your face?"

"I knew what I was doing. Scott never should have allowed you to go."

"It was a great idea or he wouldn't have."

"It was a lousy idea, and if I'd known, I would have been out of my mind with fear."

"Oh, and you weren't afraid, bound and gagged, with Hassan and his people beating you, and knowing that in the end they might kill you?"

"I could handle that."

"Well, I'm sorry, but I couldn't."

He wrapped his fingers around the sapphire and gently pulled on the chain until she took a step closer to him. "Kylie, you've got to promise me you'll never do anything like that again. Seeing you there, knowing what Hassan and his men would do if they got hold of you . . ." His voice broke. "Damn it, Kylie, *promise* me."

"Sure, I'll promise you. But only if you promise the same."

"Good Lord, Kylie," he said gruffly. "What am I going to do with you?"

She smiled up at him. "You don't know?"

He wrapped his arms around her and lifted her so that her face was even with his and her toes dangled off the floor. Then he kissed her.

"Wait," she murmured, pulling back. "Your lips."

"It'll hurt more if I *don't* kiss you."

At the first touch of her soft lips beneath his, he felt warmth ignite in his midsection and loins. "It seems like weeks since I last saw you," he muttered against her lips. "I need to be alone with you. *Now.*"

"We can't right now."

"Why not?"

She drew her head back and chuckled. "Because, David, we happen to be the center of attention."

He quickly scanned the room and saw that she was right. The music was still playing, but all the people in the room had stopped what they had been doing and were looking at the two of them.

"What's the matter with them?" he asked gruffly. "Haven't they ever seen a beautiful woman before?"

She laughed again and circled his neck with her arms. "I think it's more a case that they've never seen a man whose face looks like a Picasso painting in his black and blue period."

"Come on. It's not that bad."

She nodded gravely. "It's bad."

"It's not, but it would have been worse if Scott and the team hadn't shown up." He paused. "And I understand I have you to thank for the fact that they found me in time."

"I had help from a friend."

"A friend you wouldn't name for Scott."

"That's right. And don't you ask either," she said seriously. "I'd have to get permission from my friend first before I could tell anyone."

He damn well knew that it had been Molinari and it bothered him no end. He didn't like the fact that he was now beholden to Molinari. He also didn't like the fact that Kylie was close enough to Molinari to reach out to him for help. "Remind me to discuss that with you later. For now . . . thank you for saving my life."

"You're welcome."

His eyes narrowed slightly. "But I swear if you ever do anything like that again . . ." Deep feelings constricted the muscles of his throat. "I've already dealt with Scott about you being there, and you and I will talk about your involvement later."

She smiled. "Oh, let's not. I mean, you've already said thank you. After that, there's really nothing else to say."

"That's where you're wrong."

He felt a tap on his shoulder and turned to see Sin's eyes glittering with laughter.

"Excuse me, but that's my cousin you happen to be holding up in the air, and I must insist that you put her down immediately."

David chuckled. "Oh, yeah? And just who's going to make me?"

Sin looked at Kylie. "He sounds belligerent. What should I do?"

She grinned. "The mood he's in, I wouldn't do anything until you get reinforcements."

"Reinforcements are easy." He glanced around and suddenly every Damaron at the party was there.

Even Kylie blinked, but David still wasn't sure he wanted to put her down yet. In fact, if he had his way, he'd never put her down. She felt so damn good in his arms, all velvet and curves, meant, he was convinced, to drive him insane, with need, with love.

"All right, now, I've talked to you all about this before." Abigail's stern voice cut through the crowd. "Why are all you Damarons congregated in the center? Oh, *David*! *Finally* you're here." Several Damarons moved aside so that Abigail could get to David. "What are you doing up there, Kylie? Release David this minute."

Kylie, along with her cousins, laughed. They all knew that where Abigail was concerned, David could do no wrong. And at the same time, they also knew she felt the very same about each of them.

"Yeah, Kylie," Jo said. "Let David go. Can't you see that he's hurt?"

"I don't know *what* I was thinking of. I'll release him immediately." Kylie pushed against his shoulders and reluctantly David loosened his grip and she slid down his body until her feet touched the floor.

He swore inwardly. He should have held her away from him and set her down instead of letting her body slide down his. Now all he could think about was how badly he wanted her. Not that he'd been thinking about much else since he'd seen her this evening. He hooked his hand around her waist and pulled her to his side.

Reaching for control of his feelings, he bent and gave Abigail a light kiss on her cheek. "It's good to see you, Abigail."

"You poor boy, you've been in another scrape, haven't you?"

"Just a small one."

"Scrape" was an euphemism Abigail used for his work, because the reality frightened her too much. His work, he acknowledged, had taken a heavy toll on those he loved, but it had only been in the last few years that he'd allowed himself to see it. "I'm okay. Really."

"You've seen a doctor? You don't need any ice or anything?"

"I don't need anything. Although," he said, deciding to get her mind off of his recent "scrape" by teasing her, "I do recall someone saying I should be put in the hospital. But I told them absolutely no way. I said that your party was too important for me to miss and that I *had* to be here."

A laconic voice spoke up. "To be entirely accurate, I said you should be put in a *mental* hospital."

"Scott," Kylie said delightedly as she grabbed his hand and pulled him through a gap between her cousins. "Abigail, this is Scott Hewitt. He and David work together."

Abigail raked him with her gaze, in particular taking in his unmarred face. "Then, young man, maybe you can explain to me why David obviously did all the work."

Scott chuckled. "Well, I'll tell you, ma'am. You may not be able to see my wounds, but I guarantee you that I've got them. Earlier this evening your godson tore long, painful strips off my hide."

"Why?"

"Because," David said, drawing Kylie back to his side, "he allowed Kylie to go along on a little job he had to do."

Scott chuckled. "Allowed? There was no allowing about it. She was going no matter what I said or did. In fact, David, I'd have loved to see *you* try to stop her."

Abigail turned toward her great-niece. "Kylie?"

She held up her hands. "No wounds. Not even a scratch. I have no idea what all the fuss is about."

Abigail shook her head. "Since you're all three standing in front of me safe and sound, I don't either. Except, David, next time, dear, do try to protect your face better. Perhaps a hockey mask."

They all laughed.

"Okay, okay—enough." Abigail clapped her hands. "This is Christmas Eve. We're having a party. So let's try and have a little peace on earth, shall we? David and Scott, that means you. David and Kylie, that also means you. Is there anyone I've left out? By the way, Scott, it's very nice to meet you, and I'm so glad you came." She pointed with her cigarette holder. "There's an enormous buffet in the adjoining room. Also a bar. Wyatt and Lion will introduce you around. Make yourself comfortable and have fun."

With a hand on Kylie's waist, David guided her toward an empty corner. "Let's get out of here."

"You know we can't leave Abigail's party, at least not yet. It's too early." He groaned. "Are you in pain?" she quickly asked.

"You better believe it," he said, his tone low and husky, "but it's got nothing to do with my bruises."

She thought for a moment. "Meet me at the studio at midnight."

He slowly smiled. "Perfect."

The snow whispered down over the grounds and woods. There was very little light along the path, but David's footsteps were sure and almost silent as he tread over the newly fallen snow.

The smell of burning wood reached him and up ahead he saw the studio. Candle flames flickered in the windows. A fire burned in the fireplace. He opened the door and went in, and warmth immediately enveloped him.

Not much had changed since he'd been there seven years before, he mused. Not even his reactions. His heart was beating every bit as fast as it had that night. His mouth was just as dry.

Luminous in the pale light of the candles and moonlight, Kylie descended the spiral staircase, the skirt of her blue velvet gown trailing after her. "Merry Christmas."

"Merry Christmas," he said as he watched her come toward him, her hips swaying with unconscious seduction, her eyes glittering with a loving warmth.

"Let me help you with your coat," she said, circling behind him. Snowflakes clung to his overcoat as she eased it off his shoulders. She shook the coat free of flakes and laid it over a chair. "Okay, David," she said, her tone businesslike as she took off his jacket in the same careful way. "I want the truth. Exactly how much pain are you in?"

"It's not so bad."

She moved in front of him and began to unknot his tie. Looking down at the top of her blond hair, with its delicate silver streak, he was overwhelmed with his love for her. In so many ways, he'd come close to losing her. Even now, just thinking about it made his blood run cold.

"Not so bad?" she said, working on the buttons of his shirt. "And translated, that means if anyone else had your injuries, they would be in agony, right?"

"Only if they didn't have you to take care of them."

She shot him a look as she undid the last button. "So does that mean you're going to let me take care of you?"

"As long as we can make love while you're taking care of me."

"Making love is out. Where are the pain pills Scott told me the doctor prescribed for you?"

"I threw them away. By the way, have I told you that the sapphire looks beautiful against your skin?" "

"No," she said as she pulled his shirttail free of his pants. She held the two sides of his shirt open and caught sight of the bruises along his ribs. "Oh, David."

He pulled her to him. "Don't look. It's honestly not that bad."

"I don't believe you."

"Then let's go upstairs and I'll show you."

"The only way we'll go upstairs is if you promise to rest. You're in no shape to do anything else."

"Who says?" He swung her up into his arms.

She gasped. "*David!* Put me down! You're going to hurt yourself!"

"Kylie, the day I can't lift you, or make love to you, is the day I'll be dead."

Holding her against him, he climbed the stairs to the loft and settled her on the bed.

There was no stopping him, she thought. And truthfully, she was happy to give up trying. She wanted to make love to him as much as he wanted to make love to her. The specter of death had come too close today. She wanted, needed, to spend the night in his arms, his bare skin against hers, his pulsing sex inside her.

Her gown was tossed aside, as were the rest of David's clothes. Only her sapphire heart remained around her neck. Then, as gently as the falling snow, as exquisitely as the moon's silver light that shone down on them through the tall windows, they made love.

She was mounted atop David; he was propped up against a mound of pillows. It had been her idea so that he wouldn't have to exert himself too much. But for him, that position was just another way to show her the path to rapture.

Using his big hands to clasp her buttocks, he moved her up and down over his thick, rigid sex. She held on to the headboard behind him and rocked against him, quivering with gratification.

His mouth captured one nipple and drew it into his mouth with a force that sent hot thrills sizzling through her. Her head fell back and she surrendered to the throbbing heat coursing through her. And just when she thought she couldn't take any more ecstasy, he slid his thumb between her legs, pressed, circled, and she came apart. Phenomenal and wrenching, the ecstasy engulfed her and carried her away.

Later, he pulled her against his body. "That was better than a pain pill any day," he murmured.

She chuckled softly. "It was amazing, all right."

"Kylie?"

"Ummm?"

"You know that silver dress you had on at the warehouse?"

"Uh-huh."

"From now on, I want you to wear it only for me."

She smiled. "Okay."

Soon he fell asleep, but she stayed awake a little longer, listening to his steady breathing. Earlier that night she'd considered the decision she had to make.

Now she realized there was really no decision *to* make. She loved him too much to try to exclude him from her life ever again, even though she knew her decision would mean having to live her life on his terms. It would mean living for months on end without him. But it would also mean having nights like this, when she would be able to lie beside him, her heart bursting with love for him, her body warm and satiated.

She would be giving up a lot of the things she always thought would be essential to her life, such as children and waking up with the man she loved every morning of her life. But she would do it, because quite simply she couldn't do anything else. She loved him.

Now all she had to do was be courageous enough to live with that decision.

Christmas morning dawned bright and crisp. Kylie woke early and donned an old burgundy velour robe and some thick socks. Downstairs, she built a fire, then went into the kitchen and made a pot of coffee. Upstairs, she heard David moving around.

"*Kylie*," David shouted from the loft. "*Where are you?*"

She smiled to herself, enjoying the sound of his sleepy, slightly cross voice calling for her. "I'll be right up with coffee."

"No, I'll come down."

She carried the two cups to the coffee table and stoked the fire. David descended the stairs barefoot, wearing the tuxedo pants and white shirt he'd had on the night before, though he hadn't bothered to button the shirt. Her heart thudded as she again saw the bruises on his ribs and face. If they both lived to be a hundred, she'd never get used to seeing him injured.

He pressed a kiss to her waiting lips, then sank down on the couch. She settled herself beside him and propped her feet on the coffee table.

"Isn't the day beautiful?" she asked, nodding toward the windows.

Sometime in the night the snow had stopped. Now, with the sun on it, the snow resembled a white field of sparkling diamonds.

"Yes, it is." He swallowed several gulps of coffee, then looked over at her and gently brushed her hair off her forehead. "Good morning."

She smiled tenderly. "Good morning. Did you sleep well?"

"Right up to the time when you got up."

"Sorry. I forgot about the least little thing waking you."

"Don't be sorry. Just don't leave my bed again until I say you can."

Trying to hold back her laughter, she stared at him with mock concern. "Apparently you're more injured than we thought. Those head injuries must be giving you delusions of grandeur."

Before she knew it, his hand slipped around the back of her neck and he pulled her to him for a long, deep kiss that tasted of coffee, love, and him, an intoxicating morning mixture. When he at last released her, it took her a moment to remember what she'd been about to ask him.

"How's your pain?"

"Fine. I took a couple of aspirin before I came down."

"Good. How soon do you need to leave for your parents'?"

He glanced at his watch. "We've still got time." He looked over at her. "You're coming with me, right?"

In the years before her twenty-first birthday, she'd sometimes gone with him to see his parents and had always enjoyed herself. David's mother loved to fuss over her, and David's father loved to tease her.

"The General is expecting you," he prompted. "She said to tell you she's preparing your favorite crepes for our brunch. And don't worry. I'll get you back here in plenty of time for your family's Christmas."

Nodding absently, she sipped at her coffee, pondering her next words. "David, I didn't buy you a Christmas gift this year."

"I already have the most wonderful gift of all—you." He gave her a charming grin that warmed her all over and had her wanting to kiss him again.

"But I do have a gift for you. Something I didn't buy."

"Now I'm intrigued," he said, his tone light-hearted. "Is it something you made for me?"

"No." She looked out at the snow. "I've done a lot of thinking about you and me the last twenty-four hours and I've come to a decision." They weren't touching, but she sensed his sudden stillness and hurried on, wanting to reassure him. "I love you, David. I've always loved you and I always will." She looked down at her coffee. "Although I didn't realize it at the time, fighting my love for you this last seven years has been torturous and exhausting, and I'm through fighting it."

The coffee cup was taken from her and set aside and strong fingers beneath her chin turned her to face him. "So far this sounds like the best news I've ever heard. So what's this decision and why are you having such a hard time saying it?"

She caught his hand and held it. Up until that point, she hadn't realized that she was actually tense about the decision she'd made. But David was worth it. "I'm having a hard time because it's been a hard decision for me to make. Actually, it's been seven years in the making and I didn't really make it until last night."

His gaze was thoughtful. "It must be a pretty big decision."

"The biggest. I've decided that having you sometimes is better than not having you at all. I'm finally strong enough to let you go, and *that*, David, is my gift to you."

"To let me go?"

"Your freedom to do what you want without worrying about me. I've watched you over the years, coming and going on various assignments around the world. No one knows more than I do how much you love your work." She chuckled shakily. "It's hell on the people you love, but trying to stop you would be like clogging up your lungs. Your work is your life. You couldn't breathe without it. So what I'm giving you, with all my love, is your freedom to go off on your next assignment without guilt or worry and with the sure knowledge that I'll be here waiting for you when you return."

He stared at her for several moments. "I can only imagine how much courage and heartache it took for you to come to that conclusion. It's much more than I ever expected. It's much more than I deserve. I know what a sacrifice that decision must have cost you. You couldn't have given me a better Christmas gift, Kylie, and I'll cherish the love behind it always." Holding her gaze, he lifted her hand and pressed a kiss to her palm. "But I'm going to return your gift because I don't need it."

She shook her head. "I don't understand."

"Kylie, sweetheart, you've got it wrong. It's *you* I can't live without. It's *you* I can't breathe without."

"But your work—"

"There's one more reason why I came home that I haven't told you about yet, because I had to wait until I was sure it was final."

"Until *what* was final?"

"I came home to resign from active duty."

Her pulse began to race. She was afraid to believe what she was hearing. "You're quitting?"

"No. You were right when you said I loved my work. But I'm quitting the field missions. From now on, I'm going to be based here in the city, calling the shots for the missions. I'm going to be . . ." he searched for the right word, "a spymaster, if you will. I'll be behind the scene, pulling the strings. In essence, it's still the same work, except I'll be home every night in time for dinner with you."

Tears of happiness filled her eyes. "Has the organization agreed to this?"

He nodded. "At first they said no, which is why I

didn't tell you until I was sure. They didn't want to lose an experienced field man, not to mention the battle-experienced team of Scott and me. But in the end, I gave them no choice."

"Are you sure you can be happy staying here behind the scenes? It's not going to be the exhilarating experience of your hands-on missions."

"Being in the field is rarely exhilarating, Kylie. It's dirty, it's uncomfortable, and it's dangerous. It's also very, very satisfying when we get the job done. But I've had that part of it and it's not what I want for my life from now on. *You* are the most exhilarating experience I'll ever need. I want a home and I want children, but most of all, Kylie, I want you. I love you. You're all I'll ever want."

Tears ran unchecked down her face as she laughed with joy. "For once in my life, I don't know what to say."

"Just say yes."

"Yes." With another laugh, she brushed away her tears. "Wait a minute. I don't remember a question."

He shifted, slipped his hand into the pocket of his slacks, and pulled out a small black box. Her breath caught as he opened the box to reveal a large emerald-cut sapphire ring surrounded by diamond baguettes. "The question is, will you marry me?"

"Yes. Oh, *yes*." She held out her left hand and he slipped on the ring. "It's the most beautiful thing I've ever seen, David."

The smile he gave her reached her soul, and she could see all of his goodness, all of his gentleness, and amazingly enough, all of his love for her.

"It's not nearly as beautiful as you are, but then, nothing could be. You and I belong to each other, Kylie, in the truest, most basic way, and I never want to be apart from you again."

Slowly he drew her into his arms and kissed her softly, and with a sigh of pure happiness she returned his kiss.

A long time ago, she'd run across the hall and into David's arms, and even though she hadn't known it at the time, her future had been set then and there. Now, thank heavens, she was exactly where she was supposed to be—once again, and this time for always, in David's arms.

THE EDITORS' CORNER

With Halloween almost over, Thanksgiving and Christmas are not far behind, and we hope the following four books will be at the top of your shopping list. It's not often that you can find everything you need in one store! All these sexy heroes have a special talent, whether it's rubbing the tension from a woman's shoulders or playing the bagpipes. You may just want to keep these guys around the house!

Cheryln Biggs presents **THIEF OF MIDNIGHT**, LOVESWEPT #910. When Clanci James stepped into the smoky bar, she'd already resigned herself to what she was about to do—find sexy Jake Walker, seduce him, drug him, and kidnap him. The creep was the one sabotaging her ranch, her grandfather was sure of it. So, while he looked for clues to incriminate Jake, Clanci had to keep him out of the way. When Jake comes to, he's alone, got a heck of a hangover, and he's tied to Clanci's bed. Insisting he's not the one who's kidnapped her horse, he promises to help a suspicious Clanci. As the search for the missing horse continues, Clanci and Jake are confined to close quarters, a situation that quickly reveals their real feelings. Clanci's been through love turned bad . . . will she throw caution out the window to chance love again? Cheryln Biggs throws a feisty cowgirl together with the rugged rancher next door.

A **FIRST-CLASS MALE** is hard to find, but in LOVESWEPT #911 Donna Valentino introduces Connor Hughes to one Shelby Ferguson, a woman in need of a good man. Connor is faced with two hundred hungry people and a miserable tuna casserole big enough to feed maybe fifty, at one noodle apiece. Apparently it *is* his problem when people show up to a potluck dinner without the potluck. So, when Shelby arrives with the catering vans, Connor knows his guardian angel is working overtime. Shelby's sister just got dumped at the altar, and there's enough food to feed, well, a hungry potluck crowd. Scared of the Ferguson curse that's haunted her all her life, Shelby won't risk her heart for anything but a sure thing. And if that means a staid but secure man, then so be it. But nowhere does it say she *has* to help out this seemingly unreliable guy. Never one to desert a person in need, Shelby offers to help Connor out in restoring Miss Stonesipher's house. Donna Valentino charts a splendidly chaotic course that will lead to a terrifically happy ending.

Jill Shalvis gives us the poignant **LEAN ON ME**, LOVESWEPT #912. Desperate to escape her old life, Clarissa Woods walked into The Right Place knowing that the clinic would be her salvation. Little did she know that its owner, Bo Tyler, would be as well. Bo has his own battles to fight, and fight he does, every day of his life. But his hope is renewed when he sets eyes on Clarissa. No one had ever treated Clarissa with kindness and compassion, but when she returns it, he still has his doubts. Together they work toward making his clinic a success, but will they take time to explore their special kinship? Jill Shalvis celebrates the heart's astonishing capacity for healing when she places one life in the hands—and heart—of its soul mate.

Kathy Lynn Emerson wows us once again in **THAT SPECIAL SMILE**, LOVESWEPT #913. Russ didn't know when his daughter had chosen to grow up, but he was definitely going to kill the woman who'd convinced her to enter the Special Smile contest. When he realizes that Tory Grenville is none other than Vicki MacDougall from high school, he coerces her to chaperon Amanda in the pageant. Tory doesn't really know anything about being in beauty pageants. At Amanda's age, she hadn't yet grown into her body, or gained the confidence only adulthood can give. But Russ is determined, and a guilty Tory can't very well say no. She teams up with Russ to get Amanda through the pageant, but when he starts to take an interest in her as a woman, Tory knows she's in trouble. Russ the school jock was one thing, but Russ the handsome heartthrob is another. Kathy Lynn Emerson offers the irresistible promise that maybe a few high school dreams can come true.

Happy reading!

With warmest wishes,

Susann Brailey   *Joy Abella*

Susann Brailey   Joy Abella
Senior Editor   Administrative Editor

P.S. Look for these women's fiction titles coming in November! *New York Times* bestselling author Sandra Brown brings us the timeless Christmas story **TIDINGS OF GREAT JOY**. Ria Lavender couldn't deny she wanted Taylor MacKenzie, the ladykiller with the devil's grin, but there's danger in falling for a man she can't keep. The enchantment begun in THE CHALICE AND THE BLADE continues in **DREAM STONE** as Glenna McReynolds weaves another strand in her incredible tale of romance, adventure, and magic. National bestseller Patricia Potter brings us **STARFINDER**, the enthralling, heartfelt love story of a Scotsman and a widow caught in a web of passion and danger in colonial America. In **THE PROMISE OF RAIN**, Shana Abé delivers a tale of a woman running from a murder at King Henry's court, the handsome, relentless man sent to bring her back, and the island where their secrets are revealed—an island that just might be as enchanted as their love. Finally, Juliana Garnett presents **THE SCOTSMAN**. A fiery Scottish rebel kidnaps the daughter of the English earl who holds his brother. But he soon discovers that the woman he has stolen from her family has stolen his heart. And immediately following this page, preview the Bantam women's fiction titles on sale in October.

For current information on Bantam's women's fiction, visit our website at the following address:
http://www.bdd.com/romance

DON'T MISS THESE
EXTRAORDINARY
NOVELS FROM BANTAM
BOOKS!

On sale in October:

THE FACE
OF DECEPTION
by Iris Johansen

MERELY MARRIED
by Patricia Coughlin

THE LIGHT IN THE
DARKNESS
by Ellen Fisher

AN UNIDENTIFIED SKULL . . .
A TRAIL OF TERRIFYING SECRETS . . .
AND A WOMAN WHOSE
TALENTED HANDS
HOLD THE TRUTH BEHIND THE MOST
SHOCKING DECEPTION OF OUR TIME . . .

From Iris Johansen, the nationally acclaimed *New
York Times* bestselling author of *And Then You Die* and
The Ugly Duckling, comes her most electrifying novel
yet, a relentless buildup of suspense from the first
page to the riveting conclusion.

THE FACE OF DECEPTION

by Iris Johansen

*Forensic sculptor Eve Duncan has a rare—and bit-
tersweet—gift. Her unique ability to reconstruct the
identity of the long dead from their skulls has helped
bring closure to parents of missing children. For Eve,
whose own daughter was murdered and her body
never found, the job is a way of coming to terms with
her personal nightmare.*

*When she is approached by John Logan to recon-
struct the face of an adult murder victim, only his
promise of a sizable charitable contribution persuades
her to accept. It's a simple bargain, yet it's the most
dangerous one she'll ever make.*

*The warning signs are clear. There is the specially
equipped lab Eve is taken to, in a country inn turned*

high-tech security fortress in rural Virginia. Surveillance cameras monitor her every move. The telephones are tapped. And then there is Logan himself—by turns ruthless, charming, and desperate.

But it's too late for Eve to walk out. The skull has begun to reveal its shocking identity, trapping her in a frightening web of murder and deceit. To free herself, she has no choice but to expose that identity and to trust Logan, the man who put her life in danger, a man who may see her as an expendable pawn.

Already she has made very powerful enemies. Their only agenda is covering up the truth, and their method of choice is cold-blooded killing. To them, Eve needs to be silenced forever. Because the secret of the skull must remain in the grave—no matter who gets buried with it.

They were the perfect husband and wife—
until they fell in love

MERELY MARRIED

by Patricia Coughlin

Life for Adrian Devereau, the sixth duke of Raven, was flawless, but for one nagging detail. Try as he did to live down to his reputation as the Wicked Lord Raven, the ladies persisted in viewing him as desirable husband material. So he conceived a bold solution to foil them once and for all—he would marry a woman on her deathbed and adopt the role of grieving widower. He even found a most suitable wife: Leah Stretton, overtaken by a sudden illness while journeying to London. But with Leah's "miraculous" recovery, Adrian found himself properly wedded to a beauty as headstrong as she was healthy. Now his only chance at freedom was playing her game. More adept at writing about romance and adventure than living it, Leah could not permit a new family scandal to ruin her sister's launch into society. If Adrian played her devoted husband, she would grant him an annulment later. There was only one rule: neither of them could fall in love. Of course, rules were made to be broken.

Adrian was still savoring the praise being heaped on him by his guests when the crusty manservant who managed his household appeared by his side.

"What is it, Thorne?" he asked.

Thorne bent to whisper close to his ear. "A problem, sir. You ought—"

"You handle it," ordered Adrian, reluctant to have his amusement interrupted.

"Yes, sir. But you really ought to—"

"Not now, Thorne."

The servant set his jaw and glared at Adrian.

Adrian glared back. He understood that formal entertaining was a rarity in Raven House and a bloody strain on everyone, but Snake, the former infantryman who passed for a cook, had turned out an edible meal and a pair of feckless footmen had managed to relay it to the table with a minimum of mishaps. The least the old crank could do was *pretend* to be proper and heedful.

Instead he continued to glare. "What I am trying to say to you, Y'Grace, is—"

"Raven? Darling?" a woman's voice called from somewhere outside the dining room.

Darling?

Adrian registered the gleam of smug satisfaction in Thorne's squinty eyes just before the same intriguing female voice spoke again, this time from just inside the dining room.

"There you are." The woman threw open her arms and smiled at him as if they were alone. "Surprise, darling, I'm home."

Adrian gaped at her, frozen in his seat even as the other gentlemen at the table leapt to their feet. It was she. Leah. *His wife.*

Oh sweet Lord.

What was she doing standing in his dining room?

Hell, what was she doing *standing* anywhere?

She was supposed to be . . . well, dead.

He placed his palms flat on the table and pushed himself upright on leaden legs, only distantly aware of the expectant hush all around him.

This woman was most definitely not dead.

She was breathtakingly alive. With hair the color of blazing chestnuts and eyes like fields of clover. My God, his wife was a beauty.

His wife.

Oh sweet Lord, what the bloody hell was he going to do now?

He squared his shoulders, his usually quick wits slowed by shock. Instinct made him certain of only two things. First, if Leah Stretton was standing there calling him "darling" and apparently presenting herself as his wife, he'd damn well better start acting like a husband in a hurry. And second, when he got his hands on Will Grantley, England was going to be minus one inept, disloyal botchbag of a rector.

"Leah. My sweet," he said, forcing his facial muscles to form a smile. "You have taken me totally by surprise."

"Good." She captured his gaze and held it. "That was my intent."

The look she gave him left no doubt that she had meant to ambush him with her sudden appearance and was enjoying his discomfiture to the hilt.

But why?

Why indeed, he thought, recovering his senses. He should probably count himself lucky she'd come alone—and unarmed. Belatedly it occurred to him to wonder if the woman had brothers. Large brothers. Belatedly it occurred to him to wonder any number of things he should have considered a fortnight ago.

At the moment, however, his first order of business was to wipe the increasingly speculative looks from the faces of their audience.

Striding across the room, he grasped Leah by her shoulders. "God, how I've missed you. When you first walked in I thought I must be seeing things . . . that loneliness had driven me mad and you were but an apparition. But now . . ." He ran his hands down her arms, then up, finally sliding them around to her back to draw her closer and press her stiff body tightly to his. She blinked rapidly, signaling a crack in her composure.

Good, thought Adrian. Spring herself on him, would she?

"Now that I am convinced you are real, my own flesh-and-blood Leah," he went on, "I must do what I have been dreaming of doing since I left you in Devon what seems like years ago."

Their gazes remained locked as he lowered his head. He saw resistance flash in her eyes and felt it in her tensed muscles, but she didn't flinch or try to pull away. Had she, his urge to conquer might have been satisfied and he might have gone easy on her. As it was, he tightened his grip and opened his mouth, using his tongue to claim her the way any randy bridegroom would want to, but would doubtless restrain himself from doing before onlookers.

Adrian seldom restrained himself, and he certainly wasn't about to start now and give this presumptuous chit the notion that she had the upper hand. He kissed her hard and long, nearly forgetting that they were not alone and that it was merely a performance. His blood heated rapidly and one of his hands moved to rest on the pleasing curve of her hip, as naturally as if he had every right in the world to put it there.

When he finally remembered himself, he lifted his head slowly, watching her long, dark lashes flutter and open.

"Westerham," she said, her tone steady and audible enough for everyone in the room to hear.

Adrian frowned. "What did you say?"

"I said you left me in Westerham, not Devon. Have you forgotten already?"

Westerham. Saint Anne's. The rectory. Of course. Devon was where her *fictional* sister lived. But she had no way of knowing that, or the countless other details about her life that he had fabricated that evening. That could be a problem.

Could be a problem? He nearly laughed out loud at his own absurdity. This entire affair was turning into a debacle right before his eyes.

"No, no, of course I haven't forgotten," he assured her gently. "Though when you are close to me, it is a wonder I can even remember to breathe."

"Don't worry, darling, if you forget I'll prompt you. I happen to be a most accomplished breather."

"Yes, I can see that," he murmured, aware of the impudent glint in her eyes as she gazed up at him with seeming adoration. He released her and turned to his guests. "Please forgive my lapse in manners. I totally forgot myself for a moment."

Sir Arthur raised his hand. "Perfectly understandable under the circumstances, Raven. Think nothing of it."

"Yes, allowances must be made for newlyweds," his wife chimed in, her eyes as bright as those of a hound circling a meaty bone. "Especially when they have been separated for so long. But now, Raven, I insist you make us acquainted with this surprise addition to our party."

"Of course." He handled the introductions as succinctly as possible. Try as his overtaxed brain did, it could not come up with any way to avoid using the words *my wife* in presenting her. Though the phrases *long-lost sister* and *recently acquired ward* did flit through his mind.

The damage was done now. The best he could hope for was to limit the repercussions as much as possible. To that end he proceeded to push the chairs nearest him back to the table before any of his guests could resettle themselves.

"I know you'll understand if I beg to end the evening prematurely," he said when they persisted in lingering, inquiring about Leah's health and her journey to town, precisely the things he intended to inquire about the instant he had her alone. "I fear if sh . . . Le . . . *my wife* overtaxes herself she will suffer a relapse."

His wife slipped her arm through his. "Your concern is touching, darling, but altogether unnecessary. The doctor assures me that kidney stones rarely afflict women my age and a recurrence is unlikely."

Stones? thought Adrian.

"Stones?" exclaimed Lady Hockliffe. "Is that what ailed you? Why, you poor dear, that is a horror." She swiped at Raven with her closed fan. "You beastly man. If I were your bride I should never forgive you for abandoning me in my hour of need."

"I shall spend the rest of my life making amends," vowed Adrian, kissing the back of Leah's hand before tucking it inside his arm once more. Gently. There would be time later to squeeze the truth out of her.

THE LIGHT IN THE DARKNESS

by brilliant newcomer

Ellen Fisher

It was a complete joke to Grey that he was considered such a catch. Embittered by the death of his wife, scornful of female wiles, and completely contemptuous of any attempt to bring happiness into his life, Grey hardly considered himself good husband material. And yet, if only for the shock value of it—and to put an end to all the nagging—Grey showed up one day with a bride on his arm: an ignorant, ill-kempt, timid young tavern wench. . . .

Jennifer knew she was no one's idea of a suitable bride for the rich, elegant Grey—least of all, his. But though she couldn't begin to understand the reasons behind his caustic, tormented personality, she did know one thing. He had saved her from a life of drudgery and cruelty, and she would repay him by turning herself into a ravishing, accomplished beauty who would do him credit in society's eyes. And maybe, just maybe, in the process, he might fall in love with her just a little. . . .

Jennifer found herself lying awake in the darkness that night, completely unable to sleep. Her husband had finally noticed her, had even looked at her with something resembling new-found respect and admiration.

And now that he had noticed her, now that she had earned his attention, possibly, just possibly, he might begin to feel some sort of affection for her. Perhaps the time for Grey to mourn was finally over. Perhaps, at long last, it was once again time for him to love.

With these hopeful thoughts racing in her mind, she could not sleep. The music of the stars was calling to her. Slipping from her bed and pulling on a loose linsey-woolsey gown which did not require stays, she glided silently downstairs, only to pause at the sight of flickering candlelight in Grey's study.

"Grey?"

She moved closer to the door, seeing that his head was buried in his hands, his shoulders shaking. The words he had written to his deceased wife, Diana, darted through her mind, and she felt a slash of pity for her husband, so lost by himself but so completely unable to ask others for guidance.

Last time she had discovered Grey thus, she had only dared to peer around the edge of the door. This time, moved by an impulse she could not explain, she crossed the chamber swiftly and placed a hand on his shoulder. "Grey!" she whispered urgently. "It's all right. I'm here now."

Slowly he lifted his head, raking her face with his gaze. What she saw in his stormy gray eyes caught at her heart. Defeated, haunted, they were the eyes of a dying man.

"Don't cry," she murmured, brushing the tears from his haggard face as though he were a child. Strange, she thought, how he could be so arrogant and remote by day, yet so terribly vulnerable by night. "Don't."

"I can't help it," Grey muttered in a voice clogged to hoarseness by tears. As if embarrassed by her clear, level gaze, he lowered his face into his hands once more.

She stroked the thick black hair as he bowed his head in abject misery, wishing she could do more to ease his pain. "You mustn't feel this way," she said softly, aware that her words were woefully inadequate in the face of his agony. "Please . . ."

Grey looked up at her through red-rimmed eyes. "Ah, God," he said tiredly. "You're right. I should feel nothing, but I'm too full of emotion. All I can feel is love and sorrow and grief, churned together and swirling inside of me until I choke on it." He clutched her hand to his cheek in a gesture so childlike that a lump came to her throat.

In a moment some of his pain seemed to fade. He looked up in a way that was almost shy and studied her features in the candlelight. She thought there was something strange about the way he looked at her; his expression was intent but oddly blank, as though he were looking through her somehow. "You're very beautiful," he said at last. "Did you know that?"

Startled and shocked by his sudden mercurial change of emotions, Jennifer flushed a brilliant red and started to back away, but he caught her arms in a surprisingly strong grip. "Don't go," he pleaded in a desperate, low voice. The agony had faded from his features, replaced by something even more elemental. "I need you. You are so beautiful . . ."

She sensed that he was dreadfully drunk, but she could not pull away. His long fingers held her arms so tightly and his hopeful silver eyes held her pinned. "Grey," she said in what she hoped was a reproving tone. "Let go of me."

"I can't," Grey whispered. One of his hands released her arm and reached up to stroke the smooth curve of her jaw. Jennifer froze at the peculiar sensation of his strong, callused fingers caressing her soft skin. "I've tried, but I can't. I can never let go of you. Oh, God, I want you. And you want me too. Please tell me so."

She could not look into those brilliant silver eyes and lie. "I do," she admitted faintly. Heaven help her, it was true. There was something so blatantly masculine about him, clad as he was in a ruffled linen shirt that was open at the neck, exposing part of the solidly muscled expanse of his chest. There was something terribly compelling about his sharply chiselled features, thrown into sharper relief than ever by the faint light of the candle. Grey was more than attractive, more than handsome. He was irresistible.

"Say it," he commanded softly, eyes gleaming with something more than hope. Jennifer saw the powerful emotion in his eyes, recognized it for what it was with feminine instinct, and helplessly responded to it.

"I want you," she whispered, less shyly now.

The expression of raw, elemental passion on his face left little doubt that he returned the sentiment in full. How he could want her so powerfully, so desperately, when he had rarely even acknowledged her presence in the past she could not fathom, but it was evident that he did. She was unable to bring herself to question fate. Slightly dazed at the direction events were taking, she repeated, "I want you."

The crystalline truth of those words shocked her. She had thought herself attracted to his younger self, a man with Grey's arrogance and charm, but with Edward's passion. Somehow that man was before her now. He came slowly to his feet, staring down at her with all the passion that was his nature etched clearly on his handsome face.

And Jennifer felt the first passion of her life welling up in response. She did not struggle when his lips touched hers. The thought of struggle never occurred to her. Instead she responded eagerly, joyfully, wrapping her arms ardently around his broad shoulders, revelling in the strangely delightful sensations his caressing hands and lips aroused. Even when his lips opened and his tongue delicately stroked hers, she did not recoil in shock, only pressed herself closer to him. The taste of apple brandy on his lips was so intoxicating, his arms around her so warm and solid, that she wondered dizzily if she were dreaming. It had to be a dream. Reality had never been this wonderful.

On sale in November:

TIDINGS OF GREAT JOY
by Sandra Brown

DREAM STONE
by Glenna McReynolds

STARFINDER
by Patricia Potter

HEAR NO EVIL
by Bethany Campbell

THE PROMISE OF RAIN
by Shana Abé

THE SCOTSMAN
by Juliana Garnett

Bestselling Historical Women's Fiction

⚜AMANDA QUICK⚜

____28354-5 SEDUCTION . . .$6.50/$8.99 Canada

____28932-2 SCANDAL . . . .$6.50/$8.99

____28594-7 SURRENDER . . . .$6.50/$8.99

____29325-7 RENDEZVOUS . . . .$6.50/$8.99

____29315-X RECKLESS . . . .$6.50/$8.99

____29316-8 RAVISHED . . . .$6.50/$8.99

____29317-6 DANGEROUS . . . .$6.50/$8.99

____56506-0 DECEPTION . . . .$6.50/$8.99

____56153-7 DESIRE . . . .$6.50/$8.99

____56940-6 MISTRESS . . . .$6.50/$8.99

____57159-1 MYSTIQUE . . . .$6.50/$8.99

____57190-7 MISCHIEF . . . .$6.50/$8.99

____57407-8 AFFAIR . . . .$6.99/$8.99

⚜IRIS JOHANSEN⚜

____29871-2 LAST BRIDGE HOME . .$5.50/$7.50

____29604-3 THE GOLDEN
             BARBARIAN . . . .$6.99/$8.99

____29244-7 REAP THE WIND . . . . .$5.99/$7.50

____29032-0 STORM WINDS . . . .$6.99/$8.99

Ask for these books at your local bookstore or use this page to order.

Please send me the books I have checked above. I am enclosing $____ (add $2.50 to cover postage and handling). Send check or money order, no cash or C.O.D.'s, please.

Name _____

Address _____

City/State/Zip _____

Send order to: Bantam Books, Dept. FN 16, 2451 S. Wolf Rd., Des Plaines, IL 60018
Allow four to six weeks for delivery.
Prices and availability subject to change without notice.   FN 16 9/98

Bestselling Historical Women's Fiction

⚹ IRIS JOHANSEN ⚹

____	28855-5	THE WIND DANCER . . . $5.99/$6.99
____	29968-9	THE TIGER PRINCE . . . $6.99/$8.99
____	29944-1	THE MAGNIFICENT ROGUE . . . . $6.99/$8.99
____	29945-X	BELOVED SCOUNDREL . $6.99/$8.99
____	29946-8	MIDNIGHT WARRIOR . . $6.99/$8.99
____	29947-6	DARK RIDER . . . . $6.99/$8.99
____	56990-2	LION'S BRIDE . . . . $6.99/$8.99
____	56991-0	THE UGLY DUCKLING. . . $6.99/$8.99
____	57181-8	LONG AFTER MIDNIGHT. $6.99/$8.99
____	57998-3	AND THEN YOU DIE.... $6.99/$8.99

⚹ TERESA MEDEIROS ⚹

____	29407-5	HEATHER AND VELVET . $5.99/$7.50
____	29409-1	ONCE AN ANGEL . . . . . $5.99/$7.99
____	29408-3	A WHISPER OF ROSES . $5.99/$7.99
____	56332-7	THIEF OF HEARTS . . . . $5.50/$6.99
____	56333-5	FAIREST OF THEM ALL . $5.99/$7.50
____	56334-3	BREATH OF MAGIC . . . $5.99/$7.99
____	57623-2	SHADOWS AND LACE . . $5.99/$7.99
____	57500-7	TOUCH OF ENCHANTMENT. $5.99/$7.99
____	57501-5	NOBODY'S DARLING . . . $5.99/$7.99

- -

Ask for these books at your local bookstore or use this page to order.

Please send me the books I have checked above. I am enclosing $____ (add $2.50 to cover postage and handling). Send check or money order, no cash or C.O.D.'s, please.

Name _____

Address _____

City/State/Zip _____

Send order to: Bantam Books, Dept. FN 16, 2451 S. Wolf Rd., Des Plaines, IL 60018
Allow four to six weeks for delivery.
Prices and availability subject to change without notice.   FN 16 9/98